THE O'MALLEY & SWIFT CRIME THRILLERS

ONE LAST BREATH

Cover design by Kate Smith

Edited by GS & LW

www.ktgallowaybooks.com

ONE LAST BREATH

AN O'MALLEY & SWIFT NOVEL
BOOK 7

K.T. GALLOWAY

To Alexander Gordon Smith.
The best cheerleading brother there is. I couldn't have
done it without you!

THE SEVENTH INSTALMENT IN THE BESTSELLING O'MALLEY AND SWIFT CRIME THRILLER SERIES!

A holiday they'll never forget.

After the distress of Annie O'Malley's last case, she's in need of a bit of rest and recuperation. So her sister, Mim, books them on a flight to a luxury all inclusive resort in Spain for a break.

But what was supposed to be a chance to sip sangria and reconnect with each other after so long apart soon turns into something terrifying when a group of armed men storm the hotel and take the guests hostage.

With the help of Swift and the team back in Norfolk, can Annie and Mim find an escape route out of the resort and get themselves and the rest of the guests to safety?

Or will the holiday of a lifetime that was supposed to reunite the estranged sisters leave them torn apart forever?

The seventh and most terrifying instalment yet in one of the hottest new crime series, perfect for fans of JD Kirk, LJ Ross, Alex Smith, J M Dalgliesh, and Val McDermid.

MAILING LIST

Thank you for reading ONE LAST BREATH
(O'Malley & Swift Book Seven)

**While you're here, why not sign-up to my reader's
club where you be the first to hear my news, enter
competitions, and read exclusive content:**

<u>Join KT Galloway's Reader Club</u>

A NOTE FROM K.T.

Book seven! Never did I think, when I sat down to write CORN DOLLS, that I'd still be here so many books later. And I'm so glad I am.

Thank you to all of you who read along with me and who are cheering on Annie and Swift as much as I am.

This book was great fun to write and I hope you all enjoy it.

As always, the country is real but the places and people most definitely are not.

Grab a cuppa and let's dive in…

ONE

"IT WAS AWFUL, O'MALLEY. ONE OF THE MOST gruesome things I've ever seen." The line crackled in Annie's ear, Swift's voice cutting out. She lifted herself up from the sun lounger, slipped her flip flops between her toes, and walked back through the hotel towards the air-conditioned bar and the spot for the best phone reception. "There was blood everywhere, a trail from the back door all the way to the kitchen. There were unidentifiable *bits* on the floor. I thought I had a strong stomach, but I thought wrong."

Over the phone Swift blew out a gust of air. Annie could picture DI Joe Swift, spinning on his computer chair as he spoke, the large office behind him, the rest of their team at the desks beside him. It almost made her miss it. Annie O'Malley loved working for the Major Crime Unit in her home county of Norfolk. She loved having DI Joe Swift as her boss and the bubbly DS Annabelle 'Tink' Lock and the dependable DC

Tom Page as her teammates. But what she would love more than anything right now, was to hang up the phone and get back out to her sun lounger, her mojito, and her sister, in that order.

"Sounds terrible, Swift," Annie said, nodding to the barman who was waving a cocktail glass in his hand in Annie's direction.

"Honestly, Annie," Swift continued. "It was too much for a Monday morning. I didn't know blood could spread so far, and that's something, coming from me. It was like a nightmare."

"What did you do?" Annie asked, curiosity getting the better of her.

The barman was busy throwing the ingredients of what looked to be a potent cocktail around, shaking it up in the metal container to the rhythm of the pop music gently wafting from the speakers. Annie took herself over to the windows and gazed through the glassless openings down over the pool beyond. A few guests were gliding through the water, an older couple who had made it their holiday ritual. Two or three families lazed around the pool side. And a young couple Annie recognised as the newlyweds in the honeymoon suite of the boutique hotel were slathering each other in sun cream.

"I had to step outside and take a deep breath is what I did." Swift's huffing down the phone brought Annie back to her conversation and away from the water. "Then I went to hunt down the culprit."

Annie felt her stomach twist and pulled back to

appreciate the whirring of the overhead fan. The bar was a luxury tiki escape, held off the ground by stilts to make it authentic, and everything was bamboo, including the fan which meant every time it took a trip around its axis it made a noise not dissimilar to a helicopter taking off.

"Look, Joe," she began with a heavy heart, "if you're not up to it anymore you can't just bail on me. He's already been through too much to be shipped somewhere else while I'm away on the first holiday I've had in years."

"He disembowelled a mouse on my kitchen floor." Swift replied. "Kitchen, pantry, utility room, boot room. Not to mention the hallway and half of the living room."

"It's not Sunday's fault your house is so big that the mouse had to run a rodenty version of The Hunger Games before he succumbed to his injuries." Annie pictured Swift's Victorian turreted mansion smack bang in the middle of the city, electric gates, and huge garden to boot. "Sunday's instinct is to hunt for food, he grew up on the streets and doesn't know any better."

"What about the packets of smelly expensive cat food you've got him on? Do I need to start opening the packets and running around for Sunday to catch them too?" Swift replied, but Annie could hear the smile in his words.

"Just give him cuddles and he'll be fine," Annie said, seeing the barman placing a neon-coloured cock-

3

tail with candy floss and sprinkles on the bar. "Look Swift, some really important business has just come up here too, I need to go. Please look after Sunday and I'll be home before you know it."

There was a silence on the line and Annie wondered if Swift had already hung up. Then she heard him sigh.

"I hope so, O'Malley," he said, quietly. "It's weird here without you."

Annie's stomach took another deep dive.

"I mean," Swift added brusquely. "The *team* misses you, we all do, it's not the same here without you."

Annie could hear Tink calling something out in the background, but Swift must have wrapped his hands around his phone as she was too muffled to understand.

"Bye Swift," she said. "Send my love back to the team."

She ended the call with a smile and a shake of the head, snapping a photo of her cocktail as the barman stuck a mini umbrella in it as a final garnish and sending it off to Swift marked 'urgent business'. It may be only just past midday, but Annie was determined to relax on this holiday as much as her sister would allow her to. And if that took a constant stream of garishly delicious cocktails then so be it.

The hotel was a great find. A luxury boutique offering, set in the tranquil surrounds of the Spanish hills. It was built in a horseshoe shape with three side

4

of decadent rooms all facing the infinity pool that looked as though it was falling through the mountains and into the Mediterranean Sea. With two bars, a cafe and an a la carte restaurant, and the sounds of the cicadas chirping into the evenings, they had everything they could possibly need to relax for seven days away from work, life, and Sunday the cat who Annie had rescued from execution on her last case.

Sunday wasn't sure about being rescued, outwardly much preferring the hard life on the streets to the comfortable life with Annie, but she had seen the humongous ginger cat cuddling up to her pot plant and in the desk drawers of her office-cum-flat on more than one sneaky occasion. Swift had promised to look after him while she was away, and it sounded like he was struggling.

Sipping her drink and feeling her shoulders drop a few inches, Annie thanked the barman profusely and headed back out the bar and down the steps to the hotel corridors. Slipping through the hotel to the reception, Annie felt light on her feet as she made her way back out to the poolside. The way the hotel was positioned meant that all rooms looked over the pool, with the bars and restaurants spread over the ground floor and the bedrooms on the floor above. It was small enough to feel safe and secure, and large enough to not feel as though she was in the pockets of the young mum and her son who had arrived at the same time as Annie and Mim had, or the happily married couples who were all touchy feely in the warm, heady scents of the Med. She recognised a few to nod hello to, or small talk over the breakfast pastries, but everyone kept themselves to themselves and that was just as Annie preferred.

"Oy, Annie," Mim called from the middle of the pool. "Where's mine?"

Annie tilted her head, questioningly, before remembering the hot pink drink in her hand.

"Sorry," she said, shrugging and sipping. "Work call, I needed sustenance and was out of hands."

She held up her phone in one hand and her drink in the other, a faux sad look on her face.

Mim swam over to her and lifted herself seam-lessly from the water, flicking her fingers in Annie's direction. Annie winced at the coolness but relished it all the same. The Spanish heat was like a comfort blanket, but her cheeks were still flushed after her conversation with Swift.

"Work call, eh?" Mim said, giving her the side eye. They traversed the loungers by the pool back to their own, tucked away in the shade of a blooming Bougainvillea giving Annie's drink a run for its money with its colour. "When are you two going to admit how much you like each other and put the rest of us out of our misery?"

The rest of us. Annie took a sip to delay her reply. Her sister had only reappeared in Annie's life recently and already she was integrating herself with Annie's work life. It wasn't that Annie didn't like having Mim around, she had spent the best part of her life trying to

6

locate her, thinking their dad had absconded with her when Mim was just a baby and Annie was seventeen. It was the questions and upheaval that Mim's return had brought with it that Annie was finding unsettling.

"There's nothing to admit," Annie replied, choosing to focus on the lessor of the two evils. "Swift and I are just friends. *Good* friends."

Annie pondered her reply, knowing she was bending the truth quite a lot. She liked Swift more than she would ever admit to herself. It was a dangerous zone to enter.

"Even if you weren't my sister, Annie," Mim went on." I'd still be able to tell."

Annie sank down onto her sun lounger, the condensation from the bottom of her glass dripping on her bare stomach. She shivered and pulled a towel around her shoulders, closing her eyes to the sun overhead. Her eyelids turned pink, and the warmth on her face made Annie smile.

"See," Mim said. "Just the mention of him and you're smiling."

Mim sat down on the edge of her lounger, rubbing her short ginger hair vigorously with her towel. Annie was learning that Mim wasn't one for stillness. They'd only been at the hotel for two days and already they'd taken a trip to the hills and an outing to sample the local gin. Not to mention Mim's daily swim lengths and early morning run along the clifftops. Annie scooped a finger of candy floss into her mouth and relished the sweetness. Work kept her fit enough; she didn't feel the urge to fill her time with anything other than a paddle in the pool and a brisk walk to the tiki bar.

"I'm smiling because we're away on holiday in the best hotel ever," Annie said, reaching out an arm and taking Mim's cool hand in hers. "With my sister and a cocktail and the sun is shining. And everything is good."

Mim squeezed her hand then stood up, pulling her lounger more into the sun. Annie watched as she lay down, her young body still taut and lean and not yet saggy with age. A small tattoo on Mim's thigh peeked out from the side of her bikini bottoms, a compass with no letters. Whether it had a meaning, Annie didn't know, but it gave Annie ideas of the cult she thought their dad had enrolled Mim in and made her skin prickle with goosebumps. Mim grabbed her paperback full of sudoku and propped herself up on her elbows to tackle them.

Annie tapped her phone screen to see if Swift had replied to her message, but with no reception she had no notifications at all. She lay back and closed her eyes again, drinking in the warmth, the heady, sweet scent of the flowers shading her from burning, and the happiness she felt from Swift's words. He *was* a good friend, they had formed their companionship pretty quickly after he'd recruited Annie to their team, but did he feel more than that for her? She was too riddled with the anxiety of ruining their friendship to find out.

Mim broke through Annie's hedonism with a little thought of her own.

"He keeps himself incredibly fit, he's a great cook, he's compassionate, caring, and incredible at his job." Mim said, pen in between her teeth. "So, if you're *really* not interested, then maybe I'll have a go."

Annie's eyes shot open, and she glanced over at her sister who was grinning at her like a Cheshire Cat.

"Really?" Annie asked, her heart in her throat at the idea of Mim and Joe together.

Mim winked at her, her green eyes glinting in the Spanish sun. "Just what I thought."

And for a split-second Annie wished her sister would disappear again.

TWO

A CRASHING FROM THE POOLSIDE WOKE ANNIE A FEW hours later with a jolt. Disgruntled to be torn so rudely from a dream, she screwed her eyes tight and tried to immerse herself back into the comfort blanket of sleep. But it was no good, she was well and truly alert. Even on holiday, Annie couldn't help but stay attuned to the comings and goings around her, her job forcing her to be hyper vigilant much of the time.

Sitting up on her lounger and stretching her arms to the sky to pop out the curve in her spine, Annie was surprised to find herself alone. Mim's lounger had been moved back next to Annie's, out of the sun, but it was empty, even the fluffy towel had gone. There was no low chatter of the other guests or happy laughter of the children in the water. In fact, aside from the loud clacking of the cicada, it was eerily quiet.

Annie drew her own towel around her shoulders,

the temperature drop as unsettling as the empty pool-side. A single lilo floated across the water, pushed by an imaginary breeze. Petals from the Bougainvillea were scattered across the tiles and dotted in the water, little pink splashes of colour that should be pretty but reminded Annie of blood splatter.

Swinging around, she slid on her flip flops and stood, looking over the hot pink flowers at the rest of the pool. All the loungers were empty, a few wet towels discarded across the seats as though their owners had been scooped out of the resort by giant's hands as they lay sunbathing.

Annie felt her heart rate rise and hushed it with reminders that she was on holiday in a posh resort where she was safe, but it did little to help.

Fishing her phone from where it must have fallen under the lounger, Annie saw it was just after five, not quite dinner time yet. So where was everyone? With no reception, Annie had no choice but to head on into the hotel to try and find some other signs of life.

"Mim?" she called, breaking through the noise of the cicada, and rattling herself even more, adding quietly. "Oh Annie, get a grip."

Her flip flops slapped loudly on the tiles, the noise echoing off the water. Annie tried to tiptoe before realising that was almost impossible in shoes where the *only* grip was her toes, so she carried on, noisily around the pool to the reception. There was no happy face waiting to wish her good evening, no staff at all by the looks of things. Annie's mouth twitched, one hand gripped tightly around her phone, the other holding her towel to her chest like a shield.

To her left was the corridor leading to the steps up to the tiki bar with the good phone reception and the larger of the two restaurants. To her right, the posh bar she hadn't yet been in because it had a code of no swimwear and shoes that didn't flip and flop, and a smaller cafe. Annie didn't take long to decide to try her room instead. Heading up the stairs to the bedrooms behind the reception desk, Annie listened out for the sounds of people A laugh, a cough, a snore, but it was as though they'd vanished while Annie had been snoozing.

Swiping her keycard, Annie pushed open the door to the room she was sharing with Mim, half expecting to see her laid out on the floor doing sit-ups, or to hear the hot rushing water from the shower, but the room was as deserted as the rest of the hotel.

"Mim," she called again, dropping her phone onto her bed, and grabbing a beach dress to throw on over her bikini. "Are you in here?"

It wasn't a small room, but unless Mim was hiding under one of the two queen sized beds then chances were she wasn't there. Annie stuck her head around the door of the en-suite just in case, but the claw foot tub and the walk-in shower were empty too.

"I feel like I'm in the twilight zone," Annie said, quietly to herself in the bathroom mirror.

She pulled her hair up into a ponytail as the heat tripled the size of her auburn curls and she walked back into the bedroom. Across from the beds was a sliding door out onto a small balcony. Annie and Mim had sat out there on their first night sipping sangria and skirting around the conversations of their parents, not quite ready to dive in.

Annie slid open the door and stepped out into the heat of the evening. It was still like entering a sauna, a bank of warmth at the threshold scooping Annie up and wrapping its arms around her. The smells were intoxicating. A mixture of flora and fauna and coconutty suntan lotion made Annie pause, closing her eyes, and smiling.

Their room was in the middle of the horseshoe of buildings. Directly overlooking the pool and the mountains that stretched on either side, and the sea beyond. Annie's eyes were drawn to the pinnacle of the vista, where a cove of the Mediterranean was almost enclosed by the steep rocks, but something down by the pool caught her attention. A small boy, no older than four or five, at an uneducated guess, tottered about by the edge of the water. Glancing back and forth, Annie realised there was no sign of the boy's parents, and he was clearly enticed by the bright coloured lilo still floating gently in the middle of the pool.

"Hey," Annie called, frantically trying to get his attention as he got down on his knees at the water's edge and started to lean towards the inflatable. "Wait there."

Spinning on her heels, she skipped back out from

the balcony and sped across the apartment. Grabbing her keycard from where she'd thrown it on her bed, Annie raced out of the room and down the corridor, taking the polished stairs as quickly as she dared in flip flops.

"Wait," she cried out as she rounded the bottom of the stairs and rushed to the poolside, darting as quickly as she could to the deep end. "I'll get it for you."

But there was no sign of the boy, the pool area was as empty as Annie had left it only moments earlier.

Shit.

Annie ran around the outside of the pool, trying to see in the water, but the surface rippled as though a wind was blowing it. *Or a body had just disturbed it.*

She threw off her dress and dived into the deep end, ignoring the no diving signs, ignoring the stinging in her eyes as she pulled them open to search underwater. Twisting her body round in circles, Annie felt her lungs burn at the effort to keep them full. It was no good. She surfaced and drew in deep gulps of air, spinning herself around to try and catch sight of the young boy.

Where are you? Please be okay.

Annie felt her arms and legs weighing her down, her lungs ached, but her head was screaming at her to find the child.

"Buen buceo."

Annie startled at the voice and the little laugh that came with it.

"Hello?" she called, sweeping escaped tendrils of her hair off her wet face.

"Eres graciosa," came the voice from behind her,

She spun around to look, doggy paddling with her legs to keep her tired body afloat. A face peeked over the top of the inflatable, grinning at her with baby dimples and eyes white against his tan. It was the boy. Annie sighed in relief and felt herself sinking as her lungs deflated. Gently pulling herself to the edge, Annie waved hello to the boy, glad of the emptiness of the rest of the pool area. She had no idea what he had said to her, but the fact he could talk and laugh and hadn't sunk to the bottom of the pool was enough for Annie.

"Bomba de buceo," the boy shouted, and he threw himself off the inflatable and into the deep end of the pool.

Annie startled again, climbing out the water, looking around for his parents to come and get him and stop him from sinking. But he surfaced quicker than her brain had clicked into gear that they were still the only two around.

He swam like a fish, in and out of the water, fast, slick, darting under and shooting back out again.

"Jeez," Annie whispered through her teeth, grabbing her dress and pulling a lounger to the edge of the pool to perch on.

He may have been a better swimmer than she was,

but he was still a minor all alone in a dangerous situation, and Annie wasn't going to leave him here in the twilight zone to fend for himself.

"Where is everyone?" she asked him, as he lay on his back and stared at the sky.

"Delfines," he sang, leaving Annie none the wiser as he dived back under.

She sank down, resting her head in her hands, propped up on her knees.

"Well if the world has left just the two of us, then you're the designated fisherman," she said to the bubbles of water popping on the pool.

Just as Annie was wondering what she could bring to the survivalist party of two, the noise of chatter floated up from beyond the end of the pool where it dipped away to the sea view. Peering over the edge, she saw the heads of a crowd of people walking slowly up the hill and back towards the hotel. One bright orange head she recognised very well.

"Mim," Annie called over the wall. "There you are!"

A gate tucked away into the whitewash stone wall surrounding the hotel swung open and the poolside was once again a throng of activity. The staff made their way quickly back to the reception desk, brushing their uniforms of sand and dust. The newlyweds had a glow about them that illuminated the darkening evening, and Mim was chatting so animatedly with another woman that she barely noticed Annie until she'd nearly tripped over the lounger.

"Annie," Mim said, her eyes alight. "We've just seen the most amazing thing."

"Where did you get to?" Annie asked, feeling at a disadvantage sitting down. She pulled her dress back over her head and stood up, nodding a hello to the woman with Mim. "I was looking everywhere for you. I thought maybe I'd ended up in a Stephen King novel!"

"Ha, you and your imagination," Mim laughed. "It was a pod of albino dolphins, but one of them looked bright pink, the same colour as those flowers."

Mim pointed towards the bush Annie had slept under while all of this had been going on. Annie felt annoyance rise in her chest.

"Why didn't you wake me?" she asked, trying not to sound too irritated.

Mim wrapped an arm around Annie's shoulder and squeezed.

"You looked so peaceful," she said. "I didn't want to disturb you. And, get this, you needn't worry about missing out because I've booked us onto a dolphin watching expedition tomorrow. Sofia is coming too, aren't you?"

The young woman nodded.

"Sí," she replied in Spanish before adding in broken English. "If it's okay? Hugo and I would love to come."

"Of course," Annie smiled at the woman, taking in her tanned skin and champagne brown hair. "Is Hugo your husband?"

The woman's laughter was like crystal.

"No," she replied. "Él es mi hijo. Um… my boy."

The young child emerged from the water at the sound of his name, smiling at Sofia.

"Ah, Hugo," Annie said, waving at him. "Yes, we've met already."

He grinned at Annie and then dived back into the water. Sofia followed him, slipping out of her coverall and sliding into the water as effortlessly as her son had.

"They seem nice," Annie mused, watching them hugging in the water, Sofia wrapping her arms tightly around Hugo until he wriggled away.

"Hmm?" Mim was distracted, watching over her shoulder as two men in polo shirts emblazoned with dolphin motifs, tried to lock the gate they'd all returned through. They were talking in low voices, hushed, fast, slightly intimidating.

"What's going on over there?" Annie asked, nodding at the commotion.

"No idea," Mim replied. "The gate's broken, though, maybe they're arguing about who has to pay for the damage. I dunno. Not our problem, we're on holiday. Come on then, sister of mine, let's go dress for dinner. I think we should treat ourselves to the posh place this evening, push the boat out."

"Push the boat out," Annie agreed, nodding, her attention not quite pulled away from the hushed voices of the men arguing by the gate.

THREE

THE NEXT MORNING ARRIVED FULL OF SUN AND BLUE skies and a sticky heat that felt like it was brewing to be the hottest day of their holiday so far. Which all helped when Annie's alarm blared across the room at an ungodly hour.

"Urgh," she moaned, turning over and hitting the snooze button. "Whose idea was it to go dolphin watching in the middle of the night?"

"Up and at 'em, Annie." Mim was already showered and dressed and sitting at the end of Annie's bed looking sprightly.

"Jeez, you scared me." Annie shot up, pulling the covers over her to protect some of her dignity.

"And it's not the middle of the night," Mim went on, handing Annie a small, white cup of hotel room coffee. "It's six, it's bright and sunny, and the dolphins will wait for no man... or woman," she pondered, making her way over to the floor length curtain and tugging it open.

The sun pooled into the room, hitting Annie in between the eyes. She winced, spilling her coffee over her fingers, wincing again.

"Shut. Now." Annie ordered, screwing her eyes closed. "I'm not wearing enough clothes to be getting out of bed with the curtains open."

Mim laughed, drawing them wider. "We're on holiday, you're walking around in a bikini half the time. Besides, no one is looking into our room."

Annie reluctantly slid out of bed, clutching the coffee to her face and scurried to the bathroom.

"No," she muttered, closing the door behind her to pull on a bikini, denim shorts, and a white linen shirt. "They're all still sound asleep like normal people on a normal holiday."

———

Thirty minutes later Annie was well and truly humbled as their boat cruised leisurely out into the bay. The water was turquoise, like a picture on a post-card, clear enough to see fish in the shallows and the steep drop off where the reef ended. The white cliffs rose around them like sentinels, protecting the boat from what lay beyond, peering back over her shoulder, Annie watched the whitewash of the hotel, cleverly built to blend into its surroundings, getting smaller and smaller as they sailed further away from the shore.

There were eight people in total on the dolphin expedition. Both Annie and Mim, and Sofia and her son Hugo had snagged the best seats at the rear of the boat. Hugo knelt on the padded bench, his mum white knuckled holding onto the back of his t-shirt and Annie trailed her fingers in the water as she took in the other boaters. The newlyweds sat gazing into the open ocean, fingers entwined in each other's. Annie had spoken to them a couple of times over the buffet, *Charlie and Ricky*, she thought, wracking her brains to remember their introduction. Charlie had the kind of all over tan that came from being a frequent holiday maker, her blonde hair long and wavy and Ricky was classically handsome with a six-pack that could grate cheese.

They must have felt Annie staring at them, their heads turning in unison to look at her. She smiled, giving them a classic British grimace as the boat dipped over a wave. They smiled back, casual smiles that creased their eyes and filled their faces. Charlie lifted a hand in a wave, the other gripping Ricky's tightly as the sea started to get choppier. There were two staff manning the boat, making up the eight. Annie recognised them as the men from the previous evening, the same dolphin emblems stitched into their shirts.

"This is where the fun starts." The staff member not behind the wheel turned to face them. "It's just a short trip out to the deep, but the sea here can sometimes be a little rough."

As he spoke, the boat dipped dramatically at the bow and they all tipped forwards giving a gasp, followed by a collective giggle. How the man was still upright was anyone's guess, as he was balanced only on his two muscly legs.

"Exactamente," he added, laughing.

Annie studied his face; young, Spanish, attractive. He reminded her of a Bond baddy, in fact, they both did, something about them oozed mystery and intrigue.

"Close your mouth, you're dribbling." Mim elbowed Annie in the ribs. "If Joe could see you now, he'd burst a blood vessel."

"Oh shush," Annie replied, closing her mouth, and looking away from their captains. "It's the sun and the skin on show, and everyone here is really good looking." She whispered the last bit, not sure if Mim heard her over the rush of the boat and the splashing of the water.

Swift wouldn't burst a blood vessel because of Annie checking out the locals. The rough sea might do it though. They'd both nearly drowned in a small cave off the North Norfolk coast, swept in by a fast-encroaching tide. Annie wasn't sure how he felt about the ocean after the experience. Looking down at the water as it turned deeper and darker, Annie wasn't sure how she felt about it now, either. Goosebumps prickled her arms and she tried to focus on the here and now and not the *what could have beens.*

"He's attractive enough for *that*," Mim nodded at Annie's pimpled arms, rolling her eyes and shaking her head.

"Nothing to do with him," Annie said, pointedly rubbing her skin with her hands. "Just thinking about what could be underneath us, you know? Do they have sharks in Spain?"

"Si, si tenemos tiburones," the man said, coming to sit next to Annie. He smelt as good as he looked. "But you don't need to worry about sharks when you're here with us. We'll look after you. And you're staying out of the water, yes."

The boat gave another lurch and Annie gripped his arm as she almost lost her seating.

"I was hoping to, yes," she said, unclenching her fingers and wincing as the tan flooded back into his skin. "But now I'm here I'm not so sure."

The man laughed, not unkindly. "Samu is a great captain," he said, leaning into Annie and lowering his voice. "But he likes to keep things fun, hey. How do you say it? *Living on the edge.*"

Annie gripped her seat as the boat rocked over another rough wave. "I've come away on holiday to get far, far away from that edge," she replied.

"Then I'll make sure I'm between you and the drop." He winked at Annie, shaking her hand gently "Anders, at your service."

Anders swung himself around on the seat to face

Mim, Sofia, and Hugo, leaving Annie to the sea views and her own thoughts. In the peripheral, as she stared out across the open water, Annie could hear Anders talking in Spanish to Sofia and Hugo, the lilt of the words, the rolling of the vowels, she loved the accents and wished she'd tried harder at her Spanish GCSEs. Swift had once told Annie he was fluent in French and Spanish and she'd had to bite her tongue before she'd requested that he only spoke to her in languages much more romantic than their own going forward. She smiled, remembering the moment.

The waves were calming now they were out past the bay and onto a larger body of water. Behind them, the Spanish coastline was a hazy shade of dark blue, cloaked by mist and sea spray. Seagulls had followed their boat, hoping for titbits of picnic or fishermen's cast aways. Their loud cries echoed off the water and threw Annie back home to her small office-cum-flat in the city centre where the birds congregated at her window waiting for the day to start and the pedestrians to drop them their lunch. A sickness settled in her stomach, a longing for home, for her own space no matter how small. For the camping bed she climbed into every night, no matter how creaking the springs were. For the cat she'd rescued, no matter how stinky he was. And for the man she couldn't stop thinking about, no matter how much Annie knew she couldn't risk being honest about her feelings.

"Penny for your thoughts?" Mim placed a cool

hand on Annie's leg, drawing her back to the boat and the ocean around them.

Annie focussed on her sister. The skin on her face bronzed with the sun, freckles dotting the bridge of her nose, her green eyes a great giveaway to their sisterly relationship, the rest of her features sprung almost identically from their mother, petite and deceptively meek. Ironically, really then, that their dad chose Mim to take with him.

"When are we going to talk about our parents?" Annie said, curiosity getting the better of her. "We came away to catch up and find out more about each other's childhoods, but so far we've drunk our body weight in Sangria and talked about the weather."

Mim drew the corner of her bottom lip into her mouth and chewed on her cheek, and Annie felt the guilt gnaw at her like Mim's teeth on her skin. The younger sister nodded almost imperceptibly.

"Sorry," she said, her voice almost eaten up by the roar of the boat thundering through the water. "I've been having such a lovely time with you I haven't really wanted to bring up the topic of our parents for fear of ruining the holiday. But you're right, it was the whole point of coming away, wasn't it?"

Annie snatched up Mim's hand from her leg and held it tightly. "No, I'm sorry," she said, rubbing the back of Mim's hand with her own the way their mum had done to Annie when she was younger and needed a little comfort. "I don't know why I just said that. We're here to look at dolphins, not talk about a childhood that's left us both unable to forge friendships that last longer than a week and go deeper than the epidermis. Let's look at the dolphins."

Annie was overcompensating now and she knew it, but the hurt on Mim's face had been too much for her to bear.

"I'll tell you all I know later over dinner," Mim said, pulling her hand free and stretching out her fingers that had turned white with the pressure of Annie's love. "We can top up our blood alcohol to make it more bearable. Deal?"

Annie nodded. "Deal."

"Why so sad?" Anders asked, waving goodbye to Hugo and catching Annie and Mim deep in conversation. "Not enjoying your trip?"

Annie couldn't deal with the guilt of the handsome Spanish man too, so she spread a smile on her face and gave him her best eyelash flutter. "We were just wondering where you had hidden the rum. Surely no seafaring trip is complete without rum?"

Anders laughed, the worried lines on his face evaporating. Running a hand through his thick, dark hair he pouted and fixed his eyes directly on Annie's.

"Dolphins first," he said, his gaze not wavering. "Rum later. I get a drink made especially for you. Don't go searching about for it though, promise me. There are things on this boat that your great captain, Samu, wants to keep a secret, hey?"

He winked again and headed up to talk to Charlie and Ricky toward the bow of the boat. Captain Samu was focussed on the wheel and the ocean ahead of them, his white shirt flapping about his tanned forearms, his hair blowing in the breeze. But there was something about the way his jaw was set that made Annie's skin ripple. Swift called it her spidey senses, an intuition about others that did her well in her job with the police. Annie found it useful, the way she could tell when others were lying or hiding something by the look on their faces or the tension in their bodies. It wasn't a skill she wanted to have to call upon on holiday again, but as Samu glanced over his shoulder at the disappearing coastline behind them, she felt a stirring in her stomach that she couldn't settle.

Under his feet he nudged a large duffle bag further into the hull of the cockpit, the one Annie had assumed was full of bottles of rum, and Annie wondered what it was that Samu needed to keep a secret from his guests.

FOUR

"Dios mío, mirar, mami." Hugo cried out across the boat, his little arms flapping out to sea. "Delfín, delfín. Momia, mirar."

The boat slowed to a stop and bobbed gently on the waves. Annie stood, holding the edge of the hardtop for balance and looked in the direction of Hugo's excitement. He had spotted a pod of dolphins, their lithe bodies galloping through the waves, ducking in and out of the water, over and under each other.

Annie's breath was drawn from her body as she watched them. They looked carefree, chattering happily as they swam beside the boat.

"Wow," Mim breathed, standing up next to Annie. "They're magical."

She looped an arm through Annie's elbow, smiling up at her sister with watery eyes. Annie squeezed Mim's arm with hers and turned her attention back to the dolphins, trying not to get distracted by whatever Samu was doing down in the cabin where he'd disappeared to almost as soon as he'd switched the boat engine off. Anders stood at the very bow of the boat, balancing as it bobbed in the water, whistling through his fingers in the direction of the pod of dolphins.

"I like to think I'm their favourite," he shouted back to the passengers enthralled by the spectacle. "They come when I whistle. Look."

He popped his fingers into his mouth and let out a high-pitched sound. Annie flicked her gaze from the man to the dolphins who seemed to be jumping and swimming despite the whistle, not because of it. She raised an eyebrow at him, catching the glimpse of a cheeky smile before he whistled again.

"Anders," Samu shouted as he ducked out of the galley, jumped up and walked around to join his friend on the bow of the boat. "Our guests don't want to hear *you*. They are only here for the fish."

A giggle escaped Annie's mouth as she heard little Hugo shout what could only be *mammal* in Spanish. Ignoring the correction, Samu patted Anders so hard on the back, the poor man's fingers flew from his mouth, but they had such a camaraderie going, Annie wondered if this was all part of a well-rehearsed play.

"What, my friend," Anders replied loudly, shocked. "You don't think I can get my sea pets to do tricks?"

Samu held a hand up to shield the glare of the sun

from his face, getting a better look at the dolphins as they swooped in and out of the water.

"Wild animals," he said, gesticulating to the water. "Animal salvaje. Not friend."

Hugo was transfixed by the scene, Charlie and Ricky too. Sofia stayed sitting at the back of the boat, gazing lovingly at her son not bothering about the dolphins at all. Annie wondered if she had enough time to duck down into the cabin and have a rummage through the duffle bag.

Stop it, she chastised herself. *You're on holiday. Not on a case.*

Squeezing Mim's arm again she ignored the itch in her stomach to have a quick peek in the cabin and looked over at Anders to see him lift his hand out to the water. As though perfectly timed with his sea pets, as Anders fingers extended a sleek blue grey dolphin rose out of the water and tapped them with its bottle shaped nose, clicking loudly as though laughing, wiggling its muscly body to and fro. Hugo jumped up and down, clapping his hands and looking back to his mum for a shared moment of joy.

"Told you so," Anders laughed, watching as the dolphin flipped back into the water only to jump out again and flip over backwards with a swish of water from its tail sailing through the air.

Charlie and Ricky bore the best of the soaking, their clothes wet through from the splash, as the dolphin pod surrounded the boat and circled like a sort of sea mammalian synchronised swim team. They swooped and jumped, chattering their excitement, jumping up to all the guests to bop their hands or flick them with water.

"This is amazing," Mim cried, her fingers stroking the nose of a particularly robust dolphin with what looked like a smile on its face. "Are they actually wild, or have you brought them out here to play with us?"

Anders looked over at Mim with a huge smile on his face.

"As wild as they come," he shouted over the splashes. "They know the boat noise now. Always coming to play. They're fun, hey?"

"They're the best," Mim cried back as the pod of dolphins rounded the front of the boat and all arched out of the water on their tails.

Hugo squealed with joy again, reaching out his arms to Anders and Samu as they stood on the bow waving at the dolphins. He started to clamber up towards them, across the slippery seats where Charlie and Ricky had been sitting on the trip out, and almost as far as the wet plastic bow with no rails to hold him in. Sofia was quick as a flash, off her seat and grabbing the young boy by the back of his t-shirt.

"No, Hugo," she cried, wrapping him tightly in her arms and cradling him at the back of the boat as he wriggled as slippery as one of the dolphins. "No es seguro. Not safe."

Anders caught the commotion and was sliding off the bow and heading over to the small family. He smiled at Hugo, saying something in Spanish and pulling a funny face at the boy, who soon started laughing again. His fraught mum forgotten.

"Are you okay?" Annie asked, sitting down next to the woman whose face had paled through her tan.

She nodded, trying to smile. "Lo lamento, sorry. Overprotective. It's deep."

Annie glanced down at the dark water and shivered. Hugo may have been able to swim as well as the dolphins he'd been trying to get near, but this water was cold and deep and one wrong move wouldn't be worth thinking about.

"It is deep," Annie agreed. "You're his mum, of course you're going to be protective. Nothing wrong with that."

Sofia smiled again. Annie wasn't sure if the young mother understood what she'd said, but with her hand gestures, the implication of her words was clear. Annie was starting to wonder if Sofia didn't like the water at all. She'd looked on edge the whole trip, nervous, antsy, never too far away from Hugo. Still, if Annie had been charged with looking after a boy with a free spirit like Hugo, she'd need a stiff gin before getting *on* the boat, never mind staying cool and collected during the trip. Talking of which.

"Where's that rum, Anders?" she asked, her eyes searching the boat.

Charlie and Ricky were gazing at the dolphins as they swam away, their arms wrapped up in each other. Samu was by the wheel, clicking buttons and turning over the engine of the boat. But there was no sign of Anders, and as Annie looked from side to side, no sign of Mim either, which was strange given the size of the boat.

"Did you see where Mim went?" Annie turned to Sofia, her heart racing.

Sofia's brow ruffled as she shook her head.

"Samu?" Annie started towards the captain of the ship just as the cabin door popped open and a flushed looking Mim appeared. "Mim, god, you gave me a fright. Where have you been?"

Anders' head peeked out from behind her sister's.

"Oh," Annie grinned. "Enough said."

"Shut it." Mim flicked Annie on the arm and went to sit back down next to Sofia. "Anders was just showing me the toilet."

Annie looked properly at her sister; through the flushed cheeks her skin looked a little green.

"Seasick?" Her eyebrows raised into her sunburnt forehead.

"It's the rocking of the boat when it's not moving forwards," Mim said, head now between her knees. "My brain can't cope with the lack of control."

Annie sat down next to her with an arm over her sticky shoulders.

"That's another thing we can blame our parents for," she said, quietly, feeling the shake from Mim's laughter.

ANDERS AND SAMU HELPED THEIR CREW DISEMBARK onto a small island, no bigger than Swift's back garden. Mostly built from the whitest, cleanest sand Annie had ever seen, the island had a few palm trees dotted in the centre atop course, long grass. It was idyllic, an island from a fairy tale or a children's book. It was just what Annie would imagine when conjuring up the image of a tropical paradise. Annie hopped off the boat and held out her hand to Mim, who looked decidedly better since the front of the boat had been moored on the shore.

The six guests dispersed around the sand, Charlie and Ricky dropping onto their backs, their toes in the shallow water, Sofia and Hugo running for the trees. Annie watched as Hugo clambered up the trunk of the nearest palm, his hands and feet gripping tightly.

"He makes me tired just looking at him," Annie said, nodding towards Sofia and her son as she picked him off the tree and deposited him back onto the grass.

Annie and Mim walked a little away from the others, Mim's colour completely returning to her cheeks.

"I'm sorry I thought you and Anders were up to something naughty in the cabin earlier," Annie said as they found a spot of perfectly white sand to sit on.

As the turquoise waters lapped quietly onto the shore, Annie looked at a batch of orange coral shouldering a drop off not far from where they were sitting, brightly coloured fish darting to and fro.

"Perfectly acceptable thinking pattern," Mim joked. "I was down in the hold with a very attractive young Spanish man." She paused before adding. "Would you have minded? I've seen the way you look at him."

Annie raised an eyebrow but didn't react to the bait.

"He's beautiful," Annie said, eventually, watching as Anders and Samu dragged a couple of large bags from the boat to the shoreline, the duffle nowhere in sight. The two men were talking to each other with ferocity. Annie wasn't sure it came from her not understanding the language or an anger between them. "Very beautiful. But I'm not looking."

She saw Mim give her a side eye.

"Why?" Mim asked.

Annie drew a heart in the sand with her finger, watching as grains trickled into the divot, filling it as quickly as she made it.

"You know why," Annie said, not looking at Mim, the acid churning around in her stomach.

"I knew it!" Mim cried. "It's Joe, isn't it?"

"He has no idea," Annie added quickly. "And it's a bad idea. So don't go saying anything to him."

"Oh, he knows alright," Mim replied. "And he is pretty much on the same page as you. But my lips are sealed for as long as I can stand the two of you pussy-footing around each other like frenemies."

Annie went to reply but was interrupted by the

welcome sight of Anders and a rather large hamper of food.

"Lunch, ladies," he said, placing it in between them with a flourish and the scent of salty sea water. "No rush, we stay here for hours. Swim, rest, sleep, eat, drink. Be merry. Relax, you're on holiday."

He skipped away, bare footed on the sand. Annie watched his muscly calves tense with each step.

"Sure you're sure about Joe?" Mim asked smiling, peeling open the hamper and lifting out a bottle of champagne, the side slick with condensation.

Annie chuckled and reached for a tub of salad, ripe with tomatoes, olives, herbs, and leaves. She plucked off the lid and picked out a plump, green olive, popping it in her mouth and relishing the saltiness.

They ate like queens: salads, fruit, crackers laden with butter, olives, cheeses, and the most delicious chocolate covered fruit, washed down with cold bubbly. It was incredible to think that Anders and Samu had three of these hampers stored on the boat ready to whip out after their dolphin show.

"This is perfect," Annie said, licking melted chocolate off her fingers and lying back to stare up at the clear blue sky.

The sun shone down so fiercely that beads of sweat started forming on her stomach, trickling down to her belly button.

"Fancy a cool off?" Mim asked, wiping her own hands, and closing the lid of the empty hamper.

"How about we head under the trees instead?" Annie replied. "Mum always said it was dangerous to swim after eating."

"Did she?" Mim asked, jumping off the sand and holding an arm to Annie. "What else did she say? What was she like growing up? What's she like now?"

They were doing it now, then. Annie took Mim's hand and hauled herself to her feet, grabbing two bottles of water and heading to the shade of the trees. Ricky and Charlie were snorkelling the coral drop off, and Sofia and Hugo were playing a game of catch with Anders. Annie's gaze swept across the island, looking for Samu, but he must have gone back to the boat as there was no sign.

"She makes a mean hotpot," Annie said, sitting next to a tree and propping her back against its rough trunk. "She was attentive, growing up, always made sure I was clean and dressed and prepared for any eventuality. Packed me a lunch every day, even if I was just heading to the shops or to a friend's house. Never wanting me to go hungry. She worked hard but was always there before and after school. Made me go to college nearby so she could keep an eye on me. There was a lot of love, but it was always given from a distance, as though she never wanted to get too close. Still is. I find it hard talking to her sometimes as I have never been able to break through that outer layer. I don't blame her, really. She was overprotective and weirdly distant after you were taken."

"After we *left*," Mim corrected, sitting down crossed legged beside Annie, and taking her water. "I wasn't taken any more than you were, Annie."

Annie felt her stomach lurch as though they were still on the boat.

"No," she said. "Sorry, after so many years of being told and believing Dad kidnapped you, it's hard to remember what *actually* happened."

"I guess we were both told things that weren't true." Mim dug her toes into the sand. "That's what I find so hard to process. Why not let us have access to each other, no matter how much Mum and Dad didn't like each other."

"Maybe it was to do with what you said about Mum," Annie said, quietly, remembering the way Mim had told her their mum was a killer.

"What did she tell you?" Mim asked. "About our dad."

Annie took a deep breath and told Mim the story she'd believed from the age of seventeen. That her dad had kidnapped her sister and run off with her in the middle of the night. Taken her to a cult. Left Annie and her mum behind as though he never cared about them.

"I had my dad up to the age of seventeen, Mim," Annie choked. "Then that relationship was torn from under me. I thought he didn't love me. That he preferred you and only wanted you."

Annie felt the tears trickle down her cheeks, she felt the hands of her sister in her own.

"Dad wanted to take you, Annie," Mim said, softly, brushing a loose curl from Annie's eyes. "He told me he was going to go back for you. But that it got too dangerous, and he had to cut all ties."

It was a gut punch that Annie wasn't ready to deal with.

"What do you mean?"

"When Dad and I left, things weren't great with him and Mum." Mim puffed out air between her lips. "He never said it overtly, but I think he was scared of her."

"Scared?" Annie asked, wiping her face with the back of her hand. "Why? Mum wasn't violent to him, was she?"

Despite the boiling sun, Annie felt goosebumps prickle her skin. Her mum *was* violent, she had killed a man. Annie had no idea of the details yet, but there was no denying the truth.

"It was to do with her work," Mim added.

Annie bit down a snort. "She's a school cook. What's scary about that... except maybe their spotted dick?"

Mim laughed too, their voices rising on the salty air and travelling across the sand to Anders as he jogged towards them.

"She's not a school cook, Annie," Mim whispered before Anders reached them. "That was a lie. A cover up."

There was no time to question what Mim meant.

"Lovely to see such beautiful smiles," Anders

said, his bare chest rising and falling after the jog. "The boat is leaving, time to head home."

He held out a hand for each of the sisters and pulled them to their feet.

Annie wanted to quiz Mim more about their mum. What did she mean she wasn't a school cook. Of course she was, that's how she managed to be at home for Annie, that's why she cooked a mean hotpot.

Across the horizon, Annie could see the beginnings of a tropical storm. Dark clouds bloomed together, the mist of rain falling thickly onto the sea. Like the thoughts gathering in Annie's mind, the storm was ominous, a sign that all was not okay.

FIVE

THERE HAD BEEN NO SPACE TO TALK ON THE BOAT TRIP back to the hotel. As they'd skipped over the waves, staying just ahead of the gathering thunder clouds, Annie had kept her head down with her thoughts as Mim tried hard not to vomit over the side. And when they finally moored up at the jetty by the cove below the hotel, the six explorers looked ready for their beds.

"Ahh, sea air and excitement." Anders clapped his hands together, fighting a losing battle against the weariness of the travellers. "Good time, yes?"

Annie felt sorry for him, the smile faltering very slightly on his lips as even Hugo could only give a small whoop in reply.

"You've worn us all out, Anders," Annie joked. "Thank you for a brilliant day. It was incredible, one for the memory banks, for sure."

"Memory *bank?*" Anders raised a questioning eye at Annie.

"A lovely trip we'll never forget," she replied, helping Mim onto dry land with a groan.

"Margarita for that one." Anders nodded at Mim's green tint and she dry heaved at the mention of alcohol.

Samu appeared on the deck, one hand holding the roof, one hand gripping tightly to his duffle bag. The boat rocked up and down as the sea grew wilder with the storm and Annie felt a little seasick just watching him.

"The dinner is finished," he said to the small group of guests huddled on the jetty. "Go to the café for your meals, staff will meet you there."

Annie looked at her watch and was surprised to see it was past eight. No wonder they were all tired, they'd been out on the waters since early that morning. The sun, the salty air, the paradise island, the adrenaline rush of watching wild dolphins having incredible fun with their boat had meant the day passed in a blink. And now they were back, Annie felt like she could lie down on her bed and sleep for a week.

"Thanks, Samu," she said, feeling the weight of her eyelids. "Great captaining."

Samu gave a single nod, his eyes fixed somewhere just past Annie's shoulder with a steely force.

She gave a small wave, then turned to traipse after

her sister who looked like she could use a push up the stairs to the top of the cliff.

Stairs could be pushing it. The stone steps had been cut away into the cliff face, worn into semicircles by years of use and slippery underfoot in the rain. There were no hand holds or rails, just a rock face one side and thick, spikey brush the other which did little to alleviate Annie's fears of falling.

"You okay, Mim?" Annie called up ahead of her.

"Trying not to look down," she called back. "It was easier yesterday in the sunshine. This feels like something out of Takeshi's Castle."

"Or Squid Games," Annie muttered, looking back down to the jetty where the boat was bobbing on the rough sea.

Anders and Samu stood on the deck, watching the guests as they climbed the steps. Even in the burgeoning darkness, Annie could see them arguing again.

It's not that bad, she thought, an itching in her stomach niggling away that it might not be the steps they're arguing about.

They faded out of sight as Annie neared the gate. Propped open, the lock bent out of shape, Charlie, who had been taking the lead up the steps, disappeared out into the pool area. The rest of them followed closely behind.

It was empty apart from the older couple doing lengths in the water, their heads bobbing upright so far out of the water that their hair would be dry if it wasn't for the rain. They raised their hands in greeting and went back to their swim. Annie thought it was funny watching them glide through water that was prickled with raindrops. Though the air was still warm, she could feel the sting of the day's sun on her shoulders and cheeks. Maybe a dip would be kind of fun.

"I'm starving." Mim broke Annie out of her train of thought. "What did Samu say about dinner? Have we missed it?"

Sofie turned back to answer. "The main restaurant serving is over, but we go el café. Come now?"

Hugo was way ahead of her, already running through the doors to the hotel and speeding to the right. Annie's stomach turned over itself and rumbled loudly.

"Me too," she laughed. "It doesn't seem that long since our picnic, but I'm starved as well."

She pulled her hair from its ponytail and retied it on top of her head. Her skin felt sticky with sand, sweat, and salty air, but a quick dinner then a shower would sort her out.

The hotel felt quiet, a few staff milled about in reception, but Annie imagined most guests were relaxing after dinner before the evening entertainment started, or maybe still in the restaurant, finishing up their desserts. She was sure the bars would fill up pretty quickly too.

The smaller of the two eateries was at the far end of the corridor. It was airy, windows open to both the pool area and the cliffs on the other side. Tiled floor and dark wooden tables, with a *help-yourself* soft drinks table and a juke box, it felt like the poor man's version of the restaurant on the other side of the complex where they'd eaten all their other meals. But the smells that rose from the kitchen were enough to make Annie's mouth water and her stomach growl again, and she had little care for what the place looked like.

Charlie and Ricky took a small table by the outer windows, Sofia and Hugo just behind them. Mim opted for a table overlooking the pool and pulled out a chair for Annie.

"Thanks for today," Annie said, sitting down with a thud and lifting the menu. "That was a trip of a life-time. I can't get over how playful the dolphins were, given that they're wild animals."

"So much better than seeing them in an aquarium or a *swim with the dolphins* type set up," Mim agreed.

"They're more intelligent than the people who lock them up," Annie added, deciding on a Mediter-ranean salad and extra fries and a cold glass of white wine, a little detour from her usual Malbec.

"That's the truth." Mim put down her menu and looked over the table at Annie. "Can I finish what I started to tell you earlier?"

Annie felt like the chair was dropping out from under her; in the midst of the trip back and the sun and tiredness, she'd almost forgotten what Mim had said about their mum. Almost. There had been a pit of discomfort sitting in her stomach that she'd put down to the shiftiness of Samu, but actually maybe she'd done him a disservice and the discomfort was all her own making. She nodded, biting her cheeks, not really wanting to hear the rest of the story.

Mim leant into the table and Annie copied her, keen to keep this between just the two of them for now. She knew eventually she'd tell Swift, he was her sounding board, her confidant, but for now it felt like a secret that was to be kept within their family.

"Mum worked as an undercover police officer," Mim whispered. "I don't know if she does anymore, or how long she did it for after Dad and I left, but when we were still there, and while you were growing up, she worked in Vice."

Annie inhaled so sharply she nearly choked on her own spit.

"Vice?" She hissed. "As in, she worked on the streets?"

Mim shook her head. "I don't know. I doubt it, it's complicated."

"Too complicated to tell me about?" Annie asked angrily, before sitting back, puffing out air. "Sorry. Not you. I'm not angry at you. Why didn't she tell me?"

Mim shook her head again, reaching across the table to put her hands over Annie's.

"She wasn't allowed to tell you. Isn't allowed, I don't know. All I know is that she got in too deep and lost herself there. Dad said he couldn't tell the difference between Mum and whichever part it was she was playing."

"Dad knew?" Annie leant in again. "The whole time, he knew, and he didn't tell me either?"

"That's where they first met. Dad only left because he'd given her an ultimatum. *Leave the police or I'll leave you.*"

"WHAT?" Annie felt a ball of fury in her belly. "Mum and Dad both worked for the police? God, no wonder Mum hates what I do. How has nobody in the station said anything to me about them?"

Mim shrugged as a whistling waiter appeared at their table. Annie looked around the room, aware again of the others there, of the holiday setting, the whirr of the aircon overhead, the chirping of the cicadas through the window.

She put her order in, waving at Hugo as he sat alone, Sofia nowhere to be seen.

"God, talk about blindsiding me," Annie whispered through her teeth.

"It's hard to take in," Mim replied. "But please don't let it spoil your holiday. We knew it was going to be a difficult discussion but aren't you glad we've done it now? Started it anyway."

"I thought it would be difficult for *you*," Annie said, realising as the words came out just how selfish she sounded. How selfish she'd been. "This whole time I thought Dad was in the wrong. Stealing you away from your family. Away from me. I thought we'd be talking about *that*. I didn't realise I'd have to process just how much I'd been lied to my whole life."

Mim's forehead scrunched. "Right, so you wouldn't have come if you realised how hard it would be for *you?* Would you have even tried to find me if you knew how hard it would be to hear the truth?"

Annie felt sick, she looked down at the table, guilt stricken and dizzy. "Of course I would have."

She questioned herself in the empty silence the conversation had left. *Would I?*

There was a moment of almost stillness, as though time itself was waiting for everyone in the cafe to catch up to it. Then a bullet, faster than the vacuum of sound, flew through the air, smashing the windows beside Hugo's head, breaking the state of inertia. Another shot. Puncturing the flowers between Annie and Mim in a spray of pink petals. A thud. Annie looked over as blood sprayed from the side of Ricky's arm, hitting Charlie like a paint gun. Charlie screamed and the air rushed back into the small restaurant like a tidal wave. Bringing with it the unmistakeable rat-a-rat-a-rat of an automatic weapon being fired far too close.

Annie felt her body tense, her fingers cold, her heart racing. She looked across the table at Mim, over the room at Charlie, Ricky, and Hugo and knew that they had a matter of seconds to get to safety or the next round of bullets would end their conversation for good.

SIX

ANNIE FELT HER SENSES GO INTO OVERDRIVE AS MORE shots rang out across the hotel complex. The shooter was close. Too close. She closed her eyes, took a deep breath to steady her nerves, and switched from holiday mode to work mode. Pin prick attention, focussed, fighting the fear with adrenaline. It felt like a huge swathe of time had passed, the sand falling through the hourglass one grain at a time, but it had been merely seconds since the first bullet hit the window.

Pushing her chair out from under her in a silent slide, Annie swerved around the table to Mim and sank to the tiled floor, grabbing Mim's hand as she went. She pushed her sister up against the wall, the open window above their heads. They dropped heavily, Annie's knee hitting the tiles and pain reverberating up her leg and into her hips. Wincing, she bit her lip and blinked to clear her eyes of tears, looking across the floor to triage the state of the others. Hugo was on his own, his face blank, pale, his bottom lip wobbling, Sofia still nowhere to be seen. Charlie was huddled over Ricky a pool of blood circling them beneath their chairs.

Shit

Her brain in overdrive, Annie held her breath, listening past the sobs of Charlie to the dangers on the other side of the wall. It felt quiet, the rush of blood in her veins blocking out a sense that Annie desperately needed. Shrugging her shoulders, Annie blew out her breath slowly and quietly, before lifting herself very carefully to look out over the pool. Her eyes darting across the empty space, her brain razor sharp, she made the call. Quickly, before the shooter appeared again, she scrambled low across the restaurant floor until she reached the young child. She gathered Hugo up in her arms and shushed him like a baby. Standing where she was, in full view of the lit window, she was like a sitting duck, they both were. The pool area was still empty, but the spaces beyond were in shadows, darkened by the rain and the burgeoning evening, the giant plants beside which Annie was sunning herself not long ago, providing extra cover for a man who had death on his agenda.

Hugo was shaking, Annie could feel his terror through her arms.

"It's okay," she whispered as quietly as she could. "I've got you."

In just five steps she'd made it back to her table

where Mim had crawled to hide. Sliding Hugo down her hip, Annie squatted and nodded to him to join Mim.

"You stay here," she whispered again. "I'll be right back."

"Annie." Mim's voice was shaking. "Please be careful."

She nodded, unable to speak without giving away her own trembling voice. Annie didn't want Hugo to panic more than he was, she didn't want to risk him fleeing to find Sofia. Mim needed someone to protect her, and Ricky was bleeding out onto the floor of the restaurant. There was nothing Annie wanted more than to stay under the table with Mim and Hugo, to be as careful and quiet as she could and wait for help, but she knew she couldn't do that. Her nature was to protect, and Annie was back down on her stomach, sliding across the floor to Ricky before she could change her mind.

"Charlie, let me see," she whispered, kneeling beside the couple, her hand on Charlie's back. "I work for the police; everything will be okay. I'm sure someone has called for backup, and we just need to sit tight and wait."

Charlie looked up at Annie, her face grey, her eyes wide and stained red with tears.

"We can't wait," she said. "Ricky won't make it if we wait."

Annie felt her stomach drop out from under her. She thought he'd been hit in the arm, had hoped that it was a superficial injury and hadn't hit any of the major arteries running down from his shoulder to his wrist. But the look on Charlie's face made her think differently.

"Let me see." Annie moved on her knees to take Charlie's place next to Ricky.

The floor under her was hard and unforgiving on her body, but she barely noticed the pain as Charlie lifted her hands to show Annie the damage. The bullet had hit Ricky in the arm, just above his bicep, but nothing had stopped it piercing through the skin on the other side and lodging itself in his ribs. The pool of blood under him wasn't just coming from the wound in his arm, it was gushing out through his t-shirt with alarming speed.

Annie glanced up at Charlie and back down at Ricky, unable to hold the young woman's eye because they both knew that this wasn't a superficial injury. Ricky had been shot and without help he didn't have long to live.

Without thinking about it, Annie stripped out of her linen shirt, rolling it into a long, thin tourniquet.

"Hold this," she whispered, handing it to Charlie whose bloody hands stained the white material a vivid pink in a matter of seconds.

Annie reached over and took hold of Ricky's shoulder and hip.

"When I roll him," she said, glancing back to Charlie, "I want you to slide that underneath his chest."

Charlie was a statue, the pallor of her face, the chalky puttiness of her skin. She was going into shock, Annie needed to work fast before she lost them both.

"Charlie," she whispered a little louder. "Are you still with me?"

Charlie's eyes stayed fixed, staring off into a distance that didn't involve her partner bleeding out onto the tiles. A rattle of bullets sounded out across the pool again, the flashing light of the gun illuminating the water like a sick firework show.

"Charlie," Annie yelled over the sound of the shots. "I need you with me. Please?"

Another tirade of bullets rang out and Hugo cried out from under the table. Annie felt her legs turn to jelly, they were all going to be found and littered with bullets. Annie was never going to see her mum again, never going to find out the answers to the million and one questions that Mim had opened up in her. And then there was Swift. Annie felt her brain firing as though the light show was inside her and not out by the water. She felt heavy, her limbs too hard to lift, her eyes wouldn't focus. The sound of the bullets slowed, as though they too were falling into shock, and Annie paused, waiting for the piercing pain and the blackness.

It didn't come.

The pool area quietened, Hugo's cries falling away to silent tears as Mim cuddled him close to her chest. The noise of Ricky clawing in a lungful of air rushed through Annie's ears like a jet plane.

Shit. Focus.

Feeling like she was going to be sick, Annie pulled at Ricky's body, turning him towards her and resting him on her knees. She grabbed the shirt back out of Charlie's numb fingers and tucked it underneath Ricky's body, lowering him onto his back when it was in place.

"Argh." A gasp of pain burst out from between his blue lips.

Annie covered his mouth with her bloodied hand, shaking her head violently as his eyes pinged open wide and scared. She held a finger to her lips. *Quiet.*

Charlie was back by her side, focused and alert to Ricky's cries. Taking the opportunity of a second pair of hands, Annie grabbed the two ends of the makeshift tourniquet and pulled them tight together.

"Hold this," she whispered to Charlie, indicating the knot above the wound on Ricky's chest. "Hard as you can."

Charlie leant her body into Ricky's, he whimpered in pain as Annie tugged the shirt into place under Charlie's fingers, tying it as tightly as she could.

"That should hold the bleeding back a little," she said, with no idea if that was true or not, but the reassurance seemed to help. "But we need to move you over there. You're too visible here."

Charlie shook her head. "He can't walk."

Annie knew this was coming. There was no way

Ricky was getting to his feet and walking the few meters to the safety of the table under the window where Mim and Hugo were hiding.

"We drag him," she said, sounding surer than she felt. "I'm so sorry Ricky, this is going to hurt. You have to try your hardest to stay quiet. Can you do that?"

He nodded. The green tint of his clammy skin and the crease of his eyebrows made Annie question his reply, but he couldn't stay where he was, the view from the pool area was directly to the table Ricky and Charlie had been sitting at. If the gunman was to walk up to the windows to look inside, at least where Mim and Hugo were hiding, they were right underneath his view. Here, they'd be perfect targets.

"Take his arm," Annie whispered to Charlie. "And we pull on three. Don't stop until we're over by my sister and don't look out the windows. Even if you hear bullets we keep going. Do you understand?"

Charlie nodded, silent tears streaming down her already blotchy face. Annie took Ricky's injured hand in hers and lifted it so it was over his head, Charlie did the same with his other arm. Ricky's chest shuddered, his throat hitched, and he was biting down so hard on his bottom lip that Annie saw blood pool around his teeth.

She glanced over her shoulder out the window. It was dark now, the pool illuminated eerily with spotlights, the shadows creeping further into the corners.

But it looked still and it sounded still. It was now or never.

"Okay?" Annie looked at Charlie who looked anything but okay. "One. Two. Three."

Staying as low as they could, Annie and Charlie dragged Ricky along the tiles by his arms, outstretched behind his head. A sob escaped his mouth and he clamped his teeth down on his lips tighter than before. He was muscly which meant he was heavy, but the smoothness of the tiles, and the lubrication from the blood sliding across the floor underneath him, gave the women a helping hand. The hairs stood up on Annie's neck, not knowing what was behind her, not being able to look. She didn't like the sensation, but the task was to move Ricky, she needed to focus on that, not on the pool area and the gunman.

They dragged him around a small table for two, still set up ready for diners. Annie reached up onto the table with one hand, the other gripped tightly to Ricky's wrist, and grabbed the linen napkins that were intricately folded into swans. As they neared the table under the window, Annie felt another pair of hands reach out to her and her body felt like it had been dipped in an ice-bath before she recognised the rings and the painted nails.

"Let me help," Mim whispered, peering out from under the table, her hands wrapping around Ricky's arm and pulling.

Charlie ducked under the table, crouching low and

56

with the help of Mim, they pulled him so he was hidden from view. Annie could hear the crunch of footsteps outside and knew she only had a matter of seconds before whoever it was out there reached their restaurant windows. Sliding back out on her knees, she wiped away at the trail of blood they'd left, swiping the napkins over the tiles until the blood looked like part of the terracotta pattern. There was nothing she could do about the pool of it where Ricky had lain, but she'd masked their position as best she could.

Annie stumbled back to the table and threw herself underneath it, her heart racing, her breathing erratic. She held a finger up to her lips as the crunching footsteps drew nearer and then stopped.

The shooter was right above them and Annie preyed that she'd done a good enough job of hiding them to keep them alive.

SEVEN

THE HOURGLASS WAS STUCK. ANNIE'S LUNGS screamed with the pressure of holding her breath. Ricky's eyelids flickered as he fell in and out of consciousness, the pain from being moved too much for his body to bear.

A low cough flooded the quiet, and Annie realised just how close the shooter was to them all. Just above the table on the other side of the window. One false move and they were all dead. Mim squeezed her eyes shut and held onto Hugo in a bear hug, keeping them both as still as the night had been.

And as the footsteps sounded out again, slowly retreating from the window, Annie felt her whole body release its tension and her bones turn to marsh-mallow. She huffed out a breath, hitching more air in as quickly as she could. Through Mim's arms, Hugo looked up at Annie with hope. Annie shook her head at him, trying to give him a little smile but her face muscles were paralysed. She held a finger to her lips instead. Hugo nodded, his eyes filling with tears.

"Thank you," Charlie whispered. "He would have killed us both if you hadn't come to help."

Annie's chest shuddered as she pictured the scene. "It's okay." She turned to address them all. "But we can't stay here. The gunman will have seen the blood over there. He will know that we were in here."

"Do you think he's coming round now?" Mim asked, her words dropping in and out through her tears.

"I don't know," Annie said, relieved to be able to tell the truth. "But if he is then we need to barricade the door. Even if he isn't, we need to get that door shut and locked. And the windows too."

"Momia?" Hugo whimpered, as though he could understand what Annie had been saying. "Momia."

"I'm sure she's fine." Annie managed a smile this time. "She'll be safe in her room, I'm sure."

Sofia must have nipped out to use the bathroom. There was a small set of toilets for guests to use round by the main restaurant but Annie guessed Hugo's mum had gone to her room which would have been quicker. She hoped Sofia had locked the door and hidden when the shooting had started. The gunman hadn't yet made his way into the building. Not yet. Not unless there was more than one of them.

Annie needed to know more. She pulled her phone out of the pocket of her denim shorts, her bikini top not doing much to protect her from the freezing air con in the restaurant, her skin puckered with goose pimples.

"Shit," she whispered, sliding it back in her pocket. "No reception."

If the gunman was walking around the pool and entering the building, they didn't have long before he made it down to the end of the corridor and their hiding place.

"Mim, Charlie, can you both move okay?" she asked, watching as Hugo wrapped his arms closer around her sister.

"I'm fine," Charlie whispered. "Sorry about earlier…"

Annie held a hand up to stop her, shaking her head. There was no need for apologies, and no time either.

"Mim?"

Mim ducked her chin towards Hugo, raising an eyebrow.

"Okay," Annie agreed, though it would be tough with just two of them. "You stay here. Keep Hugo quiet and make sure if Ricky wakes, he doesn't call out."

Mim's lips thinned, her face trembled. Annie sucked in air again, wanting to gather Mim up in a hug and tell her everything would be okay.

"You can do this," she said, instead. "You're Mim O'Malley, courageous, beautiful, caring."

"Really bloody scared," Mim added with a tearful smile.

"We won't be long." Annie stroked her sister's cheek and turned to Charlie. "Can you lock all the windows on this side of the room? Quiet as you can."

Charlie nodded, though her brow was as creased as could be.

"On my signal." Annie pulled herself out from under the table, her knees were stained red with Ricky's blood.

She lifted herself up slowly at the windowsill, looking back and forth across the space. The gate to the sea path was wide open, thrown to its max, the lock still dangling from its hinges illuminated by the single strand of fairy bulbs dangling above it. An uneasy feeling dropped in Annie's stomach and settled there. Further across, the blue of the pool had darkened by the shallow end, redness blending the water to a deep purple around a large mass that bobbed on the surface.

With a sinking feeling, Annie remembered the older couple doing lengths as they'd passed for their dinner. It seemed like another lifetime ago. Her nose fizzed with tears at the thought that they were no longer together, they'd seemed so happy. Puffing out a breath, Annie kept looking. It was still, the rain had lessened, no longer blurring the air like a painting, so Annie noticed the movement in the reception. It was a man, tall, broad, dressed all in black, a hood or hat covered his hair and face. Out in front of him was a gun, the type Annie had only ever seen on the television; complex, squat with a long barrel. The type that could spray out bullets faster than people could run from them. She knew it had sounded like an automatic weapon, but seeing it made her blood chill.

The man was facing away from the pool, pointing the gun at the reception desk, swaying it back and forth. Annie said a silent prayer and thanked an invisible entity she didn't really believe in when the man turned left and started off down the other side of the hotel.

"Now," she said to Charlie. "Go, close them quietly and lock them if you can."

Annie sped out from under the window and kept low, hurrying across the restaurant to the other side. She pushed the windows closed and slid the locks through their facings. On the inside of the glass they were shuttered, the wooden types that folded open and closed again. Annie had been considering these for the lower part of her sash windows back in her office flat, and for a split second she forgot where she was and what was happening, focusing instead on the intricacies yet simpleness of the shutters. The reality snaked its way back in and she almost doubled over with fear.

There were four windows on either side, and as the two women worked quickly to shut them the room grew quieter and colder. The noises of the rain and the pool and the cicadas locked out. The air of the fans locked in. Annie shivered, pulling the shutters closed on the last window on her side. Looking over, Charlie had done the same and was sliding back down under the table to hold Ricky close.

The smells of the restaurant grew around Annie. Her stomach twisted with emptiness and fear. She wasn't hungry anymore, but lack of food would mean she wasn't able to focus, and neither would anyone else trapped in here with her.

The door to the restaurant was closed but not locked. Annie listened out for the heavy footsteps of the shooter and tiptoed over to it, her heart in her mouth. Twisting the handle down, she pulled the door slowly towards her, peeking out the smallest gap she could make. It was as though nothing had changed, even though the world was a different place from the one it had been thirty minutes ago. The lights shone down on a sparkling clean floor, music piped out from hidden speakers in the walls, and framed paintings of the famous Spanish coastline coloured the walls. Annie couldn't see around the far corner of the hallway to the reception or the posh bar, so she clicked the door closed and looked for a way to lock it. The keyhole was empty and there were no bolts or deadlocks.

Shit.

The door was flush with the wall on its right, to the left was a table replete with lemon water and bowls of fruit and breads.

"Charlie," Annie called in a loud whisper. "Help me move this to block the door."

Charlie scrambled out from under Ricky and the

63

table, her feet now bare of shoes, and ran across the room to Annie.

"You take that end," Annie instructed, nodding at the far end of the table. "And we'll lift it across the door."

Charlie moved and grabbed the wooden lip of the table. Annie grabbed the other end and together they lifted it off the floor, groaning at the weight. Annie's arms shouted in complaint, the table was heavy, the contents tilting precariously, threatening to fall to the floor and alert the gunman of their presence.

"Steady," Annie groaned. "Just a bit further."

Without the golden glow of the sun and the huge smile that had been plastered all over Charlie's face all day, she looked no older than a teenager.

"It's going to be okay," Annie continued. "We'll hide out here until we're saved. Ricky's wound is packed, he's bleeding less, he'll be okay."

They both knew it was a lie. Annie could tell by the way Charlie's face screwed up when she said it.

"He's all I've got," the young woman whispered, tears dropping from her cheeks onto the table.

Charlie's arms buckled with the emotion and the table wobbled towards the door, the water cooler toppling on its edge, the lid flipping open, water sloshing onto the tiled floor. There was nothing for it, the water cooler was going to fall and smash on the tiles. If the shooter didn't know they were there already, he'd know for sure if that happened.

Annie swung her end of the table to the door,

banging it loudly, pushing the glass bottle back upright. It tilted precariously in the other direction, thrown by the momentum, Annie's heart leaping into her mouth. It balanced on its lip, neither falling nor righting itself, until it thumped back down onto the base with a thud.

Charlie looked on in terror, eyes wide, lips trembling.

"Sorry," she said, sniffing. "Sorry."

"Put it down now, Charlie," Annie said, quietly. "This is far enough over."

She needed to get them away from the door in case the gunman came back and shot through the wood.

"Hide," Annie continued. "Quick now. Back under the table."

Charlie didn't need telling twice, she scarpered back to the others, ducking under the table with a sob. Annie closed her eyes and listened for footsteps, trying to keep her breathing steady and calm, which was hard when the blood was pumping around her body faster than an Olympic swimmer. Blocking out the sounds coming from her own body, Annie listened to the far away hammering of gunfire, screams of those caught in the crossfire. She hoped that the table was giving enough protection, because whoever was doing this had made his way around to the main restaurant where the other guests had been finishing up their desserts.

Clearing her throat, Annie gathered up some fruit

and rolls from the table in front of her and hurried back to her sister and the others.

"Here," she said, dropping the food inside their hideout. "You all need to eat to keep up your strength. We're tired, probably a little sunburnt after today, the last thing we need is to slip up because we're hungry too. Adrenaline will only last for so long and then we're going to crash. Force it down if you have to. I'll be right back."

She rushed back to the table and filled a jug with lemon water, carrying it back as steadily as she could, sipping from the brim as it sloshed over the side. Ducking down, Annie crawled under the table and huddled up next to Hugo and Mim.

They all ate in silence, nibbling the intricately woven bread and slices of mango and pineapple, swallowing it as though it were laced with arsenic and not the offerings of a five-star all-inclusive retreat. Annie felt the food clog in the fear in her throat, sipping more water to force it down, knowing that she was going to find as much energy as possible for what she needed to do next. Knowing that she'd need to find as much energy as possible to even *suggest* what she was going to do next.

"Mim," Annie whispered, working up the courage. "I need to get to the reception desk and phone for help."

Mim's face fell, she shook her head, eyes filling. "No way, someone will have already done that."

Annie looked at Ricky, his head in Charlie's lap.

66

The rise and fall of his chest was shallow, quick, the breath of a man who didn't have a lot of time left before it stopped moving at all.

"I can't take that risk," Annie said eventually, turning back to Mim. "I'll be careful. I promise. The corridor to the reception is too open. If he was to come looking for us, there'd be nowhere to hide. I'm going to climb out the window and I need you to shut it and lock it behind me."

"I'm sorry, Annie," Mim said, tears flowing heavy down her face. "I'm so sorry for what I said before. I know you would have come looking for me whatever the implications."

Annie kissed her own fingers and stretched over Hugo to place the kiss on Mim's cheek.

"I'd say this is an implication too far," she joked, smiling at her sister. "Next time you let *me* pick the destination."

Mim spluttered a laugh through her tears and followed Annie out from under the table.

EIGHT

THE RAIN HAD STOPPED, LEAVING BEHIND AN unsettling stillness and quiet. As the damp evaporated almost immediately into the warmth, the scents of the flowers, the pool, and the suntan lotion from the hours past, mingled together in the air. Annie ducked down into the shadows under the window and waited to hear that Mim was locking it behind her and pulling the shutters closed too. Ahead of Annie was the pool, a black portal of thick tar in the night. The body lay still in the shallows, no tide or wind to bob it about. It was indiscernible who the body belonged to, in death we're all the same, no individual posture to recognise or gestures to give us away. Annie shuddered, wrapping her arms around her bare skin. Though it was dark now the air was still thick with heat, but she wished she had on more than a bikini top with her shorts.

Over past the left of the pool, where the water was

deep enough that Annie wasn't able to stand, was the gate. The fairy lights flickered above it, illuminating the steps she'd walked up that evening. Annie had a huge surge of panic, her body clawing from the inside, begging her to run back down those steps and flag down a boat from the jetty or swim around the cove to safety. But she couldn't do it, not with Mim still in danger. Not with a man who was bleeding out and a boy who was scared and alone.

And you don't know who's down there.

Annie stopped breathing, listening to the voice inside her head reminding her of the broken gate latch, the argument between Anders and Samu there last night. She shook her head to rid it of questions.

The hotel was secure, the front door a key card lock, discrete high fences all around the perimeter. Even where the cliffs fell away into the sea and no one in their right mind would be able to climb up them and into the hotel, there was fencing just in case. That gate and its steps down to the jetty were the only entrance not secure, and unless it was a guest already checked into the hotel running wild with an automatic weapon, then Annie's best guess was that the gate was the point of entry.

"Shit," she whispered. "Shitty shit."

Keeping low to the ground and in the shadows and cover of the full blooms, Annie scuttled across to the gate. She slid her phone out of her pocket checking just in case she had any bars, but the signal was still non-existent, and snapped some photos of the broken latch. It had been bent right back so that the bolt no longer fitted in the sliding. She brushed away some fallen leaves and petals from around the gateposts, no idea what she was looking for but trusting enough in her instincts to know when she saw it.

Spideysenses working overtime? Annie heard Swift talking in her head as clear as though he was there with her under the fairy lights by the gate.

She wished he was. He'd know what to do to keep everyone safe. Though he'd probably barrel into the gunman and topple him over with not a care for his own safety. A sob hitched in Annie's throat and for a split second she was glad Swift wasn't there. He'd probably be dead already.

Brushing away the last of the foliage from around the gate, Annie spotted a long plastic handle, purple, difficult to see. She pinched at it with her fingernails and drew it out, scurrying back into the shadows and away from the gate.

Turning it over in her hands she saw it was a spade from a child's bucket set, the scoop had been broken off. It could be a coincidence, a toy discarded because it no longer worked. But that didn't sit right with Annie. She tucked it behind the bush she was hiding in the shadows of, in case she needed to come back and examine it later, and steeled herself to move away from the possible safety of the jetty and towards the reception and the gunman.

Nearly at the entrance, another spurt of shots rang

70

out over the water, screams following not long after. Annie heard the gunman shouting, too far away to make out the words, but the anger in his voice was as clear as day. Her hands automatically covered her head, throwing herself down to the ground, she started shaking. Bile rose in her throat, burning and hot. She needed to move; though she was hidden in the shadows, there was still too much open ground between her and the doors to reception. If the shooter came back along the corridor and out of reception, he'd walk straight into her.

She peeled her arms away from her head and hurried across the entrance, the light from the reception bright, stinging her eyes after the relative darkness of the poolside. Down the other side of the pool, where Annie had been sunbathing only yesterday, the shadows were thicker and there were more places to hide.

Think, Annie scolded herself. *How can I get into the building without drawing attention to myself?*

She knew there was the huge opening to reception, lit up like Blackpool illuminations. Coming at it from this angle had turned out to be just as dangerous as sneaking down the corridor from the cafe she had left her sister in. There was nothing to hide behind, nothing to protect her if the shooter came back from the other side of the complex. She was stuck between a rock and a hard place with a bullet slowly carving her name through the air.

"Shit," she whispered again.

A rustle of bushes, the stuttering of a breath. Annie flung herself to the floor, as low as possible, and moved further back to the wall and crouched as low as she could under the tiki bar. There was someone out here with her. She felt her heart trying to beat its way out of her chest wall like the creature from Alien. It was taking too long for her eyes to adjust to the darkness from the bright light she had been looking at near reception. She was blinded.

"Hello?" A quiet, shaky voice came out of the darkness. "Is there somebody there?"

It was female, a slight accent. French maybe, or Belgian. Annie reassessed the risk and crawled towards the voice.

"Hello?" she whispered back, trying to work out who was hiding and where.

"We're here," the voice replied.

Annie heard another rustle and saw the dark outline of a waving hand. She got up onto her feet and tiptoed towards it. There, behind a hedge in the far corner of a flower bed, hidden against the wall of the hotel, were the two older guests Annie had seen swimming.

"Oh, thank god," she cried quietly, dropping back to her knees beside them.

They were huddled together, towels wrapped around their thin shoulders, bare feet sunken into the earth around the small hedge.

"I thought…" Annie stopped herself from saying about the dead person on the water. She didn't need to

72

scare them anymore than they already looked. "I'm so glad you're both okay. What happened?"

The man looked across his wife at Annie, his face pinched, the wrinkles deeper than she remembered them being.

"We had finished our swim," he said, his accent thicker than the woman's. "And were at the outdoor shower rinsing off. We heard shouting and the sound of gunfire and one of the staff motioned for us to hide behind the shower wall. He saved our lives."

"Did you see anything?" Annie asked. "Did you recognise the shooter? How many of them are there? Anything at all that might be helpful."

They both shook their heads and Annie felt her hopes stifle.

"It happened so fast," the woman said, clutching at her husband's hand and holding it tightly between her own as though if she let go he'd fly away. "We ducked as soon as we were told to. The wall blocked anything from our view… thankfully. We'd be dead if he'd seen us. What if we'd still been swimming?"

Her voice hitched and she quietened.

"I think there were two," her husband added. "Gunmen, I mean. There was all the commotion up near the top of the pool; shots, screaming. But when we snuck out from hiding behind the wall there was another man near the gate over there, he must have been a different man because the shots were still going inside the building. He had this huge duffle bag. It looked heavy. Do you think it's full of weapons and ammunition? What if he's got a bomb in there?"

Samu.

"I don't know," Annie answered truthfully, ignoring the screaming in her head that if she'd just followed her instincts on the boat then maybe none of this would have happened. "But if it was more ammo, then you need to stay as hidden as possible. Hopefully help is on the way but I need to get into reception to use their phones."

She looked over to the brightly lit reception and chewed on the inside of her mouth until it tasted like old pennies.

"There's a door," the old man said, catching Annie's attention with a cold hand on her arm. "Behind that tree, next to the tiki bar. I've seen the staff using it, I think it's so they can move about discretely, you know?"

Annie nodded. "Where does it lead? Is it locked?"

"I've used it a couple of times, the toilets outside the main restaurant are right next door." He looked down at his bare feet. "My bladder isn't what it once was and it's a long walk around through the hotel."

He looked back at Annie, a small glimmer of a smile in his eyes. The toilet block near the large restaurant was down a corridor with a janitor's cupboard at the end. Near enough the reception to make it worth her while, and maybe there would be a phone by the cupboard.

"Five, five, four, oh," the man went on. "You'll need to key C first to clear the lock."

"Thank you," Annie said. "Please stay here and stay covered. If this isn't over when the sun starts to come up, then try to make your way back to your room. Or the toilets. Lock yourself in. Keep your feet up and I will try my best to get help."

Annie got back to her feet, still crouched as low on her haunches as she could, though the muscles in her legs were not happy about it. She took a breath and started to creep away in the shadows.

"Wait," the woman whispered after her. "Please tell us your name."

Looking back over her shoulder, Annie saw the fear in their eyes. "Annie."

"We're Ellis and Faith." The woman's bottom lip wobbled. "Pleased to meet you, Annie."

"I'll see you soon, Ellis and Faith. Be safe." The sinking feeling in Annie's gut returned, but she swallowed it down and moved towards the tree.

In the wall behind the palm, hidden so well there wasn't even a door handle, Annie found the opening. Beside it was a small keypad, backlit softly against the darkness. She keyed in the code that Ellis had given her and winced as it clicked open, the sound like a chainsaw in the quiet night. Pushing her fingers in the gap, Annie pulled the door towards her, peering inside to get her bearings and make sure it was safe. Ellis was right, the door opened up next to the janitor's cupboard, hidden away down the small corridor near the toilets. Further along, light pooled into the corridor from the main thoroughfare, but here she'd be hidden and protected from the gunmen for a little longer.

Steeling herself, Annie slipped through the gap in the door and clicked it shut behind her.

NINE

INSIDE THE BUILDING, THE SOUNDS OF LIFE FLOODED her ears. Whimpering, crying, the shouts of someone too petrified to hold it in. A chair or a table leg scraped across the floor with the squeal of metal on tiles. It was cooler on this side of the complex, too. The frigid air from the aircon trapped inside the closed windows and doors. Goose pimples scattered their way up Annie's arms lifting the hair on end as though she was about to be struck by lightning. She shuddered, clasping her hand over her mouth at the sudden rush of air escaping her lips.

Through the sounds of terrified people, there was one voice that was rising above. Angry, violent. Annie still couldn't make out the words, but the aggression was palpable. If this was one of the gunmen then he was definitely in the large restaurant at the far end of this side of the complex. He sounded focussed on whatever he was shouting at his victims, the way his words stuttered across the night. Annie knew that she could use this distraction to sneak out of the corridor and down to reception and the phone.

But what about the other gunman? Was it Samu? A man with a duffle bag. Though this was a hotel, Annie didn't imagine there'd be many Spanish men with duffel bags hanging around by the pool. And what about Anders? Was he in on it too?

There was no other option. Annie was going to have to make a run for it. If she came across the other gunman, then maybe she could hide in the tiki bar. There she'd have phone reception and could call out for help. It was a risk though, the windows in that bar were more open to the pool area, it was small, and there was only one entrance and exit up the narrow steps to the door.

Come on, O'Malley, make up your mind.

Forcing herself to stick with her original plan, Annie slid her feet out of her shoes and silently tiptoed to the end of the corridor. She looked both ways, heart hammering in her chest. Her mouth felt dry and sticky, every breath lodged in her throat, swallowed down with a tickle. The restaurant door to the left was closed, but Annie could still hear the angry shouts of who she believed to be the gunman filtering under the threshold.

"¡Dime!, o te arrepentirás."

Her Spanish wasn't good enough to translate what he was shouting, but the words provided cover for her to sneak out and head down the corridor to the right, towards reception. With the sound of her own heavy breathing rattling in her head, Annie padded across the tiles. It was just a few more footsteps to the bar.

Maybe go in. Call from there.

Annie wasn't used to feeling so unable to make a decision. But then Annie wasn't used to hiding from a gunman intent on shooting innocent holiday makers. The bar might be the quickest way to call for help.

She approached the steps up to the door, a bamboo facia had been attached to enhance the tiki effect, and from memory the door swung both ways. She could slip inside but then there was no way to barricade herself in safely. A sob bubbled up in Annie's throat from the depths of her body. She didn't know what to do, she couldn't make up her mind. And it was this kind of indecision that got people killed.

What's Spidey telling you? Swift filtered in through her thoughts again. *Listen to your intuition.*

Annie knew it wasn't actually Swift saying these words, he'd be telling her to get back under cover and stay safe, but it was what he always asked her when they were thinking about a case. *Use your intuition, O'Malley.*

Her intuition was telling her to run past the reception desk and up the stairs to her room to lock herself in. But it was also telling her to get to the nearest place she could call for help. And now that was the tiki bar.

She ran up the steps then, with one hand on the

door, Annie forced herself to be brave. She was going in. Except, as she pushed the door a fraction, letting the sounds of music from the bar permeate the quiet corridor, a loud whirring noise clicked into gear across the hotel and the whole building fell into darkness.

Oh my god!

For a second, time stood still. Darkness engulfed Anne like a suffocating cloak. She felt around with her fingertips, trying to get her bearings. Screams and cries flooded the corridor, gunfire silenced them with its rapid hammering.

Oh god, no.

Another series of clicks sounded out and an eerie orange light emanated from floor level along the corridor. Everything glowed like a horror movie. Still poised at the door, Annie pushed, halting only when the ear biting noise of scraping metal came from behind it. Whether it was someone inside pushing a chair to get to the door, or a barricade Annie was pushing away with the door, she didn't wait to find out. Lifting onto her toes, she ran as fast and as silently as she could back down the steps to the corridor and the reception beyond and threw herself over the desk onto the floor. Hidden.

The backup lights didn't quite reach the space in the circle of desks, instead it pooled under the hatch casting shadows under the surfaces. Annie shuffled back into the darkness as far as she could go, trying not to give in to the abject terror stabbing her right in the solar plexus. Her whole body started to shake. Not the kind of trembling that had encumbered her since she gave her shirt to stem the flow of Ricky's gunshot wound, but a whole-body shudder that rattled and bashed against the drawers beside her. It was the shock, she knew, but that didn't make it any easier to control. Annie was incapable of stopping it, she had to ride it out, tears streaming down her cheeks, casting her lips in a salty tang.

As time passed and Annie understood that no one was coming for her, the movements started to slow. Exhaustion passed over her, heavy and all encompassing. All she wanted to do was curl up and fall asleep, for someone to tuck her in and tell her everything will be okay. But there was no one. Her mum had lied to her, her dad had left her, and her sister was trapped in a room with a dying man.

You're okay, O'Malley, there was Swift again. *Just a little setback. We all have them. Do you remember the time I almost got blindsided by a psycho schoolgirl? Or how I came unstuck because a cat maimed a mouse on my kitchen floor? Seems trivial now, doesn't it? But it didn't at the time, and you always managed to talk me down, so I'm repaying the favour. Now, you still need to call for help. Let's see if those phones are connected to the backup generator.*

From the small trickle of orange light, Annie's eyes had almost adjusted to the darkness. She could make out shapes close by; a chair, the outline of a computer above her. Anything further out was still covered in a blanket of darkness, but from memory, the desk under which she was hiding had a phone right next to the keyboard. Annie remembered passing the receptionist on their way into the hotel that first night. She'd smiled brightly at the two sisters and waved hello, even though she'd been in the middle of a conversation with someone else on the phone. Annie had marvelled at her friendliness and waved back. Mim had been too busy trying to find the free welcome cocktails.

It had been a while since Annie had heard any shouts and she swallowed down the sickness that came with the memory of the shots fired when the lights went out. She pushed away from under the desk and swivelled up onto her knees, her joints aching with tension. From here Annie could see down both of the corridors. One way to her sister and the rest of the dolphin group. The other to the gunman and his captives. The pool stretched out in front of her, no longer up lit around the edges or fairy lit at the back, just a black expanse of nothingness. And behind her, the stairs rose into darkness. She didn't want to stay with her head above the pulpit for long, if she could see out, the gunman could see in.

Scouring the desktop, Annie spotted a phone beside a notepad, names and dates and numbers scrawled on the paper. In a different time, these names may have been coming to stay here, people waiting patiently for their holiday with no idea of the horror playing out at the hotel. Pushing the pad out the way,

Annie reached for the body of the phone and dragged it towards her. She lifted the handset and listened for a dial tone.

Nothing.

Tears fought their way into Annie's eyes, her nose stinging with the pressure.

Come on. Please.

She hammered at the controls, trying to call out, to connect the phone, to keep the hope burning in her chest, but it was no good. The phone was dead.

Sinking back to the floor, heavy hearted and all out of ideas, Annie kicked out at the chair in frustration. It flew across the inside of the reception desks, the wheels rolling silently on the floor. Annie winced, covering her ears with her hands, wishing she'd thought about what she'd just done before she kicked the chair. It was going to hit the other side of the desks, loudly. But it didn't, it bounced against something soft and came to a slow halt rolling back towards Annie.

And in the gloom at the far end of the desks, in slow motion as the world around her stopped turning, the outline of a sitting person tipped to the side and fell in a crumpled heap on the floor.

It was too much for Annie. She cried out, covering her mouth tighter, trapping the noise in her head which made it louder, popping at her ears. She scrambled to her feet, needing to get as far away from the body as she could. Maybe it was the woman who'd smiled at Annie and Mim on their first day, or the friendly guy who used to blow kisses at Annie when she'd head up to her room to change for dinner. Whoever it was didn't deserve to be lying on a cold tiled floor with their family yet unaware of what had happened to them.

Not even looking to see if the corridors were empty, Annie shot out of the hatch and into the orange glow.

Which way?

She wasn't going to go back towards the guns. Not now. She needed to be with her sister, Annie didn't want to die alone. Darting around the desks, Annie made her way towards the corridor when above her footsteps rang out on the stairs.

Shit.

Annie wasn't a swearer, but she was forgiving herself for letting them slip out in a constant stream under the circumstances. Spotting a large potted plant under the curve of the stairs, she threw herself towards it and hid out of sight. She looked up, watching, her blood running cold as a set of boot-clad feet rounded the landing and started down towards the reception area, a gun clenched tightly in his hands.

There was no escape now. Annie was going to have to wait it out behind the plant and hope that whoever it was working with the gunman in the restaurant didn't see her.

TEN

I<small>F</small> A<small>NNIE</small>'<small>S</small> <small>HEART BEAT ANY HARDER IT WAS GOING TO</small> burst right out of her chest. Blood pumped and thrummed through her body, her fingers felt swollen and tight, her whole face hurt. She often used to wonder why people froze in dangerous situations, but now she knew. Not that Annie was a stranger to putting herself at risk, she'd confronted more than her fair share of danger, but somehow she'd always managed to think straight and talk her way out of it.

Not now.

Her brain had never done this before. Her mind unable to cope. Annie could barely draw breath in through her lungs without focussing on the hows and mechanics of it.

The footsteps grew louder and the man dropped from the last stair to the reception, gun raised, sweeping the space. One false move and Annie was going to get a bullet between her eyes. He wore dark clothes, covered from head to toe, his face masked by dark glasses and a bandana. Hair poked out from under his hat, but in the orange glow Annie had no idea what colour it was.

He moved silently across the reception, sweeping his gun back and forth, back and forth. It looked like a hand gun, different to the automatic weapon that the other shooter was armed with. It was only when he turned to look out over the pool that Annie saw the bag slung on his shoulders. It was Samu's duffle, she was sure of it. He was wearing it like a rucksack, an arm thread through each handle, but the design of it was almost unmistakable.

The man muttered something under his breath and pulled off his hat to run a hand through his hair. She spotted the mussiness, recognised the forehead. Annie had been right, the man stalking the corridor was the same man she'd spent the day on the boat with. Captain Samu. Nothing about him now made Annie feel he was a person responsible for looking after the safety of others. All that had been a ploy. Maybe the whole thing was a ruse to get into the hotel in the first place. He'd been at the broken gate, he'd stood there looking at it, arguing with Anders about it. Was he the one who did it? Was he arguing with his friend about fixing it because he needed the access to the pool?

It all seemed plausible. But Annie couldn't work out the why. What could have made Samu so angry that he'd shoot at people he had just spent the day with?

"Vamos!" Samu's hushed voice cut into the silence of the night, popping Annie's ears.

He hadn't shouted the word, he'd uttered it at barely more than a whisper, but the way her body reacted it felt like he'd screamed it at the top of his voice.

He paced again, up and down the reception area like a caged animal. Annie had never felt someone's frustration ooze out of them and fill the air as much as Samu's was now. It was suffocating, clawing at Annie's throat. She had a desperate need to run, to leave the safety of the potted tree and belt it out of the open doors to the pool area. If she could just douse herself in the freezing water the feeling of being trapped would melt away.

What's he waiting for, O'Malley? Why is he pacing.

Annie caught Swift's question on her tongue, a reply not far behind.

"I don't know," she answered in her head. "What makes you think he's waiting for someone?"

Look at him. The way he's searching the corridors, gun out, not standing still for even a moment.

"Agitated?"

Yes, but it's more than that. Look closely at the way he's moving. What is he telling you?

Annie wanted Swift to give her the answers but as he wasn't real and hiding behind the plant with her, that was impossible. But her mind was obviously trying to tell her something and she needed to work out what.

Samu huffed out a breath, sweeping the gun across towards the stairs, the muzzle pointing right at Annie for a split second. She squeezed her eyes shut, hoping she'd live long enough to open them again. But Samu didn't see her. He didn't even look like he was searching for her.

"I've got it," Annie shouted in her head. "He's not looking."

You're spot on again, O'Malley.

"And if he's not actively looking for people to shoot then he's either found his primary target or he's on the search for something else?"

I knew there was a reason I signed you up to the MCU. Brains and beauty, O'Malley. Brains and beauty.

A rare smile grew on Annie's lips, there was no way Swift would say that. Her overactive imagination was giving her a confidence boost and she was all over it.

Concentration back on Samu, Annie watched him as he stepped back up the first few stairs and back down again. She watched him check one corridor, then the next, head darting around the corners to check for danger, to check for guests who might want to overpower him. But from the stillness that had permeated through the hotel when the lights went out, Annie wondered how many of them were still able to fight back.

Almost without warning, Samu grunted in frustration and stomped out the open doors to the poolside. Annie's insides squirmed liquid with fear for Ellis and Faith. She hoped they were hidden in the shadows, still and quiet. Samu m+oved out of the light from the doorway and was soon swallowed up by the darkness outside.

Do you think you can make a run for it?

"But I haven't called for help."

There's another solution.

"So tell me what it is?"

You already know. Go, O'Malley. Now.

Annie didn't need to be told twice. Keeping low and behind the cover of the reception desk, she crept around to the edge near the corridor to her sister. Peering around the corner, Annie searched for signs that Samu was coming back. It was too dark to see, but it felt quieter now, she couldn't feel the presence of another person. The entrance to the corridor wasn't far from where Annie was crouched, four meters maybe. But it was far enough to be seen. And it was light enough, even with just the emergency generator lights, to spotlight her to anyone standing outside and facing towards the hotel.

"It's too risky."

What choice do you have?

"But if he sees me, I'm dead."

And if you stay here, you're dead.

"God you're annoying."

I'm not real, O'Malley. You're the annoying one.

Annie felt sick, she was crouched here arguing with herself while Mim was scared, Hugo was without his mum, and Ricky was dying. She'd come out to try and help them and had so far managed to walk in a huge circle and achieved nothing.

Not quite nothing, O'Malley.

Annie ignored the voice, focussing on the ground she had to cover to reach the corridor. Even then she wasn't home free. There was nowhere to hide once she got there, not until she was back in the cafe. But Swift was right. She was dead if she stayed here.

With sweating palms, Annie lifted herself up to peer over the desk. The room was empty. The pool-side too dark to see. Without thinking about it, she squeezed her bare toes on the tiles and pushed off towards the cover of the corridor.

A shot rang out, Annie felt her stomach drop out from under her and threw herself across the room, flying through the air for the last two meters of her journey. She landed with a heavy thump on her knees and elbows, pain shot through her body, a gasp burst from her lips before she could stop it. Dragging her screaming limbs across the tiles, Annie pulled her back against the wall, using the only thing she could find for cover. The thin console table wasn't going to keep her hidden for long, if at all. Atop the dark wood was a basket of apples, ripe and juicy. She'd taken one not even twenty-four hours ago, marvelling at how fresh it had tasted. Now all Annie could taste

90

was the sharp, throat burning acid of an empty, churning gut.

Barely daring to look, Annie cast her eyes downwards at her skin, waiting for the bloom of red as the blood from the bullet hole seeped to the floor. She'd heard others say that being shot hadn't been immediately painful, more like an ice needle piercing a hole in the skin. Nothing happened. No delayed pain. No blossoming petals of blood. Annie felt her sides, running her hands across her neck and her legs and her neck, lifting her shaking fingers to inspect them for blood when they came away damp. But it wasn't blood, it was sweat.

The shot. It had rung around the reception as though the bullet had taken flight there. But thinking back now, Annie wasn't sure it had been quite so close. Could it have been the first gunman? Locked away in the restaurant. Either way, she wasn't hanging around to find out. Scrambling back to her feet, her knees bruised and swelling rapidly, Annie moved to the door to the cafe.

"¡Vamos!" Samu's voice filtered in through the window beside her and she froze. "¿Dónde has estado?"

Footsteps scuffled on the ground just the other side of the wall. Clear as day through the open window. Not just one set, but two.

"¿Está sucediendo?" The other voice belonged to a man. Annie recognised it almost immediately. Anders.

"Sí Sí." Samu was getting agitated. "Vamos. No hay tiempo."

Wishing she'd studied harder in her Modern Foreign Language class at school, the only word she could translate was Vamos, *come on, hurry,* and that wasn't from school, rather from watching cartoon episodes of Dora the Explorer tucked up in her office camp bed when she couldn't sleep.

Was this it then? Was Anders the first gunman? Had they done what they'd come here to do and now it was time to flee? Had Samu and Anders really committed the worst atrocity imaginable and were now heading back to their boat? They had access, they had a form of getaway. Annie didn't know what their motive was, and she didn't know either of them well enough to guess.

But something gnawed at Annie's insides, a feeling that she couldn't place Anders at the scene of a massacre. The sounds of gunshots. The screams. The dead body slumped in reception. Could the young man who'd joked and laughed with Annie and Mim on an idyllic boat trip really be involved?

Annie didn't need telling that people could be deceptive, she'd been on a few dates with a man intent on injecting bubonic plague through the veins of his victims, but there was something that didn't sit right. Samu, on the other hand. He'd been secretive and pretty monosyllabic.

The footsteps retreated from the window. Annie waited until they were barely audible and leant up to look outside. Scanning the poolside, she still couldn't make out as far as the gate where the boat would be moored. But there was a movement in the corner of her eye on the other side of the poolside. It was the two men. And they weren't heading back to their boat at all. They were coming back inside the hotel, and from the looks of it, they were heading directly for Annie.

ELEVEN

Annie didn't hang around to see if her predictions were true. Scrambling to her feet, she ran the last few meters of the corridor to the blocked up entrance to the cafe and knocked as quietly as she could on the door. Glancing behind her the corridor was still empty, but that might not last for long. Sweat trickled down Annie's back, pooling in the waist band of her shorts. She shivered, the fear still ripe in her senses.

"Mim?" she whispered through the door. "It's me. Let me in."

She held her ear against the wood, listening for sounds, for the relief of the table being moved or the sweet reply from her sister. But there was nothing.

She glanced back over her shoulder again. Still empty.

"Mim." Annie knocked once more, hoping they

could hear her but not wanting to draw attention to herself with no cover and nowhere to run to.

The orange lights beneath her feet flickered, plunging the corridor into fits and starts of darkness, like strobes at a rave. Annie was thrown back into a deeply repressed memory of lightning flashing glimpses of an old case she'd worked on with Swift. A boarding school with secrets buried so deeply they nearly overshadowed the real crime going on in front of their noses. The only way she'd seen through them was the ability to separate fact from fiction, a skill Annie thought she'd inherited from her dad through early years of playing games of Who's Who? and Blind Man's Bluff.

That's it.

With the hope that their dad had played the same games with Mim as he had done with her, Annie lifted her knuckles to the door and tapped out a rhythm.

Shave and a haircut.

Shave and a haircut.

It was the same sounds her dad had knocked on the walls and doors to trick her into walking towards them, blindfolded, arms outstretched.

Glancing behind her again, Annie saw shadows moving the orange lights around like ink on water.

Please, Mim. Please know it's me.

There was a shuffle behind the door. Footsteps maybe, or the table being lifted out of the way. Annie heard the sound of the handle turning and the door swung open to reveal a pale but very welcome Mim.

With no time for pleasantries, Annie ducked inside and slid the door closed silently behind her, finger to her lips to indicate the danger of making any noise. Carefully, Annie and Mim took an end of the table each and lifted it over the door. As they placed it back down on the floor the handle rattled and the door shifted slightly towards them, blocked by the heavy table and the weight of Annie and Mim as they pushed in the other direction.

Mim's eyes widened in fear.

It's okay, Annie mouthed, nodding, feeling anything but okay.

But the door stilled, and the sound of footsteps retreated away from them. Annie took a moment to breathe, inhaling a full lungful of air for the first time since she'd set foot in the cafe for dinner. Her head span, the lighting in the room was lower than the corridor and the relative darkness gave off the feeling of safety even if it didn't really offer it.

Mim wrapped her arms around Annie's neck and sobbed quietly into her shoulder.

"We heard the shots not long after you left and thought you'd been caught." Mim was shaking. "Don't leave us again. I can't cope."

Annie glanced over Mim's shoulder to the others still hiding under the table. Ricky looked like he was already gone, his skin the colour of putty, eyes closed, unmoving. Hugo huddled as far back as he could, hugging his knees, rocking on the base of his spine.

"He's not in a good way," Mim said, noticing Annie's line of vision.

Annie wasn't sure which of them she was talking about, it could be either of them.

"Any sign of Sofia?" she asked.

Mim shook her head, taking Annie's hand and leading her back under the table. The room was stuffy now the aircon was off, with the windows closed and the door shut, under the table felt a few degrees warmer than the rest of the cafe. Annie felt her lungs restrict and cleared her throat a couple of times before she settled back against the table leg and tried to calm down.

"What happened?" Charlie looked at Annie with eyes rimmed with red and puffy. "When's help arriving?"

The young woman was stroking her partner's hair which was slicked back with sweat. A single lock kept fighting the grain, bouncing back upright each time Charlie's hands lifted. It would be comical if it wasn't so tragic. Annie looked at her own feet, bare and dirty, unable to look back at Charlie to deliver the bad news. She was surprised to see they were bleeding. Her soles ripped at the heels, shards of something white embedded in the dirt glowing like glitter. Annie uncrossed her legs and straightened them in front of her. She was in enough pain without adding *broken ceramic vase in soles* to the list. It must have happened when she was enclosed in the darkness of the reception. Perhaps the bullet had shattered the display flowers as well as the staff.

Swallowing down the sickness at the horror of the memory, Annie shook her head.

"The electricity went off before I got to reception."

"What about other people? Is there anyone out there? Any staff who can help? What about Ricky?" Charlie was beside herself, her bottom lip wobbling as she tried to remain still enough to not wake him. "Did you do nothing while you were out there except go in a circle and then lead them straight back to us?"

"She put herself in danger to try to help," Mim hissed, she had straightened up, squaring her shoulders at Charlie. "What did you do, hey? Nothing. Don't have a go at her because the phones were switched off. Look at her, she looks like she's seen a ghost, and you're not helping matters."

Hugo looked out from where he was wrapped in Mim's arms with flaring nostrils and threw his hands over his ears.

"No pelees," he muttered over and over under his breath. "No pelees."

Annie didn't understand the words, but she could tell from the way he was retreating into himself that the anger between their small group was scaring him more than he already was.

"I saw the old couple from the pool," Annie interrupted, holding a hand up to both her sister and Charlie.

"Oh," Mim cried, hands over her mouth.

"No, no." Annie shook her head, trying to draw enough energy to smile. "They're okay. They're hiding in the gardens."

"Oh thank god."

"Did they know what had happened?" Charlie asked, going back to stroking Ricky's hair, the anger seemingly dissipated as quickly as it had risen.

Annie relayed what the old couple had told her about the shooter and the second person with the bag while the others listened on intently.

"There's more," she added, finishing her story with the key code and the guests trapped in the restaurant with the gunman. "When I was in reception I saw one of the shooters and it's Samu from the boat."

Hugo started sobbing.

"What?" Mim's face crumpled in disbelief.

"It can't be," Charlie added. "He was gruff, but he wouldn't kill people, would he? Why not just drown us when he had the chance if that's his aim?"

"I don't know," Annie replied, wondering the same herself. "But it was definitely him. Remember the bag I'd mentioned on the boat, Mim? I think it must be full of ammo. He had a handgun though, not an automatic, so we may have more of a chance against him."

"What do you think they're doing?" Mim asked.

"I don't know, but there's more," she added. "Anders joined him just before I made it back here.

Whatever it is they're after, they're not going to stop until they find it."

The image of the bodies in the pool and the reception hit hard and Annie felt her eyes fill with tears. She swiped them away with the back of her hand and tried to regain her composure. If she lost it now, there was no way she was clawing it back.

Hugo shuffled under Mim's arms, his face pale and drawn.

"Papi me salvara," he whispered before throwing his face into Mim's top and sobbing as quietly as he could.

Annie knew enough this time to know that Hugo was calling for his dad to save him.

"Is his dad here?" Annie whispered to Mim. "Did Sofia mention him?"

Mim shook her head. "I don't think he is, but he'll know where they are maybe? He might get worried when he can't get hold of them, maybe he'll call the hotel."

"And if he can't get hold of the hotel enough times, he might try the police?" Charlie added, her face alight.

"It's a possibility," Annie said. "But we can't rely on it."

Charlie blew out a puff of air, her eyes narrowing. "What do you suggest then? Because so far it's not worked, has it? And why should we listen to you anyway?"

"Annie saved your life," Mim reminded the young woman. "If it hadn't been for her, you and Ricky would have been gunned down the moment the shooter walked past the windows, so wind your neck in."

Annie thought Charlie might jump over and force Mim's own neck a little if it wasn't for her half dead boyfriend lying in her lap.

"It's okay," Annie said to Mim. "You're right for questioning me, you don't know me, I don't know you. But, like I said when you were in shock, I work for the police back home. It's just nature to try and help."

Charlie's face paled even further and she looked down at Ricky's head, stroking his hair a little too fast.

"Sorry," she muttered.

"Don't apologise," Annie said. "You're right. I didn't get help when I was out. But I do know now that we need help and we can't run. For a start Ricky won't be able to, but also, with the electrics out, the doors are locked shut and we don't know the override code for the external doors. We're in the middle of nowhere with no means of escape. So our best bet is to wait it out until help gets here."

"Do you think staff called for help?" Mim asked, cuddling Hugo tightly.

"I think the gunmen targeted staff initially, for the very reason that they didn't want them calling for help," Annie replied, quietly. "But, I have an idea. There's phone reception in the tiki bar, we can't get in from the doorway, it's blocked off. But we can try the windows. I'm going to call Swift and ask him to help us. But I'll need a boost to get in the window, it's too high to climb."

Annie looked at Mim who nodded, her whole body shaking with fear.

"You can give me a leg up and then come straight back," Annie added, filling her pockets with dried fruits from the earlier stash and then shuffling out from under the table.

Mim drew her lips into her mouth and nodded again. She was quiet, and even in the short time Annie had been reacquainted with her sister, quiet wasn't a word she associated with her. Mim started to extract herself from Hugo, lifting his arms away from her waist. He held on like a limpet, and when Annie leaned in to help, he let out an almighty wail.

"Shhhh," Mim called to him, cuddling him back in and rocking the boy to comfort him. "It's okay, I'll be right back."

Her words shook as much as her hands did.

"You stay," Charlie said, slipping out of her cardigan and cushioning it under Ricky's head instead of her lap. "Just keep an eye on Ricky for me. Keep trying to get him to drink the water. He needs to stay hydrated."

"But I…" Mim tried to argue but she was interrupted by the young woman.

"It's fine. If Hugo is going to make that noise, I'd rather be out there. You're better with kids than I am."

Charlie shuffled out of the safe space and stretched to the ceiling, groaning as her joints clicked.

"Lead the way, Annie," she said, her face set. "I'm right behind you."

TWELVE

Annie pushed the window closed behind her and Charlie and they ducked down beside the wall, hidden in the shadows. With an acute sense of déjà vu, Annie swept her eyes over the pool area to check for danger.

"It's so dark out here," Charlie whispered.

"There's no back up lights," Annie replied, closing her eyes momentarily to try and get them used to the blackness.

"Good for us, I suppose. I'm sorry I was off back there, I'm so worried about Ricky."

Annie opened her eyes, the pool area more shades of grey now than a blanket of black. She took Charlie's hand in hers and squeezed gently.

"You've got nothing to apologise for. Right, are you ready to move? We're aiming for the other side of the pool, but it means sneaking around near the reception entrance which is the last place I saw Samu and Anders."

"Oh god," Charlie whispered. "I'm so scared. I don't want to die. I'm only twenty-three, I've just gotten married."

"Charlie, listen to me," Annie said, trying to sound brave. "I'll do my best to protect you, but if we see them coming out here then you run back to the cafe window and get inside to safety, do you hear me?"

"I'm not going to leave you," Charlie hissed back.

"I'm not taking you out there unless you agree to what I just said," Annie hissed back, remembering so many times when Swift had said the same to her, and she'd been as stubborn as Charlie was right now. God, Swift must have been so frustrated with her.

"You're not taking me anywhere, I'm an adult."

They were getting nowhere arguing like this and Annie felt a little silly now, Charlie was right, she could make her own decisions. Annie tucked away that argument for the next time Swift said it to her and gave Charlie a single nod.

They stole across the lawns, around the front of the pool and safely past the entrance to the reception. It was quiet, no sign of Anders or Samu. There was also no sound from the main restaurant, no shots or cries, though Annie wasn't sure she would hear them from out here.

Ducking down under the stilts of the tiki bar, they caught their breath.

"Stay here," Annie said, still breathing heavily.

She tiptoed to the edge of the bar and around the

building to Faith and Ellis' hiding spot. They were still there, huddled together to stay warm. Annie slipped the dried fruits from her short pockets and handed it over to Ellis.

"Sorry it's all warm and squashed," she said, as they grasped her hands in thanks. "But I thought you'd be hungry by now."

Ellis passed his wife the majority of the fruit, keeping a few dates for himself and nibbling them slowly as Annie carried on talking.

"I had no luck calling for help with the hotel phones so we're going to get into the tiki bar and use my phone."

"We saw a man fiddling with the electric box," Ellis told her, pointing in the direction of an old fuse box on the back wall next to where the pool fell away to the sea. "He met up with another man by the entrance over there, but it was definitely him as they went out when he was there. Good luck, young lady."

Anders.

"God speed," Faith added, as she took dainty bites from a dried apricot. "We heard the shots and thought you were dead. There's been nothing since then, a few single shots but it doesn't bode well for all those inside, does it?"

"They may have been warning shots, to keep people quiet," Annie replied with a heavy heart.

She said her goodbyes and sped back to Charlie, trying not to picture the families she'd seen playing by the pool, the other couples on honeymoon, the parents escaping for a well-earned break. If there had been no noise since the rain of bullets after the lights went out then Faith was right, it didn't look good for any of them.

"Everything okay?" Charlie whispered, as Annie ducked back under the stilted bar.

"Yeah," she replied. "Ellis and Faith, the old couple hiding out back there, they saw Anders tampering with the electrics before the lights went out."

Charlie whistled through her teeth. "Why do you think they're doing it? He seemed so lovely."

Annie shrugged. "That's what I need to find out. We have no way of getting to safety at the moment, so our best bet is figuring out if this is targeted or a random attack to highlight a terrorist group."

"And if it's the latter," Charlie added tentatively. "Then we're doomed?"

Annie bit her lip. She didn't want to say it, but the young woman was right.

"Any movement while I was away?" she asked instead, nodding in the direction of the reception.

"Nothing." Charlie's head was haloed by the glow from the back up lights. "Do you think they're gone? It's been quiet for a while."

"No." Annie shook her head.

The silence was worrying her. It had started as a gut punch about what had happened to the other guests, but the more it went on, the more Annie's senses were telling her it was something much more

107

than that. Something the gunmen were planning together. Something big.

"So how do we get in?" Charlie asked, her attention to the roof above her.

"There's open windows just above us," Annie pointed upward, towards the wall of the bar that faced out over the pool.

"You want a leg up?"

Annie chewed the inside of her cheek, the cicadas chirruped loudly, the emergency generator must be outside too as it was like a steam train, and the waves from the sea were crashing into the cove below.

"I think we might be able to move a couple of sun beds and climb up on them," Annie replied, making a call for them both. "Then we can both get into safety."

"Okay," Charlie agreed. "So you're alright with me coming with you then?"

Charlie gave Annie wry smile.

"Sorry," Annie said. "I know you're an adult. You can make your own decision; I was just trying to keep you safe."

Charlie put a hand on Annie's arm.

"I appreciate it," she said. "But the love of my life is back there bleeding to death, and I will do anything I can to save him."

"Then let's go and call the cavalry."

They crawled out from under the bar, checking the coast was clear. With no sign of the gunmen, Annie and Charlie snuck to the nearest sun bed and lifted it silently. It was heavy, wooden with an adjustable back rest, and it took them a few moments to balance it carefully between them. Stepping around the potted plants and the low decorative walls, they placed the bed under the windows.

Annie lifted herself up onto the bed, high enough to see into the windows but not quite high enough to lift herself in. She peered into the window, expecting to see a group of guests hiding under the tables, just as her group had been in the cafe, but it looked empty. Her chest constricted painfully at the thought of what could have happened to them.

"Can you get in?" Annie heard Charlie whisper and withdrew her head from the window.

"Not without a struggle," she replied, casting her eyes over the pool area for another nearby sun bed.

Charlie jumped up next to Annie and offered her a leg up, her hands crossed together, bent at the knees.

"Up you go, then help me when you're there." She shook her hands to speed Annie up. "At least this way we're not giving them easy access to the bar too."

Annie didn't have to think hard about the proposition. Out the corner of her eye she saw movement in the reception area and the silhouette of two men in the frosted window walking towards them.

"Quick," Charlie whispered, the desperation ripe in her voice as she looked over her shoulder and saw the same thing.

Annie stepped into Charlie's hands and grabbed

the windowsill, hauling herself over it and onto the sawdust floor with a clean sweep. With no time to check out her surroundings, she picked herself off the floor and leant out the window for Charlie. Grabbing her around the arms, Annie used all her strength to lift the young woman off the sun bed and in through the window on top of her. Charlie rolled off onto her back on the floor and they both lay panting, listening for the sounds of footsteps or gunfire.

It was even darker in the bar, the low orange glow of the emergency lighting not present and the limited lighting from the pool area not enough to lift the shadows of the room. The two women lay for what felt like hours to Annie; she lifted herself onto her elbows, the imminent threat of the men no longer heavy on her shoulders. Her skin crawled with the sawdust as it stuck to the sweat on her back and arms and legs, and she felt the heat of the day in the bamboo walls around her.

"You okay?" she whispered to Charlie. "Give it time for your eyes to adjust and we'll move to somewhere a little safer."

Through the gloom, Annie could hear Charlie's rapid breathing.

"Listen," the young woman said. "What's that noise?"

Annie tried listening harder but the blood travelling around her body at ten times its normal speed wasn't helping.

"Hello?" Charlie spoke louder now. "Is there someone here? Annie, can you hear that rustling?"

Annie held her breath, sitting upright and focussing her attention on the room. From somewhere to her left she could hear the ticking of a clock, immediately beside her was Charlie, still breathing like a stream train. And there. Far enough away to not be clear, Annie heard a scratching noise.

"What's that?" Charlie continued. "Annie, do you think it's one of them?"

Her voice was barely audible, carried on her breath from her lips to Annie's ear.

Annie needed to check out the room, make sure they were safe, ideally, she would have done it before Charlie climbed in the window but there hadn't been time for that.

"Stay here and keep still," she whispered back, grabbing Charlie's hand and giving it a squeeze.

Annie got to her feet, brushing her hands of sawdust so she could feel properly for the furniture around her. She closed her eyes, trying to get her bearings. They'd entered by the window overlooking the pool, the room was littered with tables and chairs, brightly coloured ornaments and feathers and Hawaiian garlands even though they were in Spain. The bar was on the back wall near the door that Annie hoped was still blocked.

Feeling her way along the wall, Annie manoeuvred around the tables towards the door to check it was still safe. The scratching sound was getting louder, Annie's whole body fizzed with the idea she was walking towards something large and hairy, because the noise didn't seem human.

Not one to shirk away from wild animals, Annie carried on around the room to the door. Up close she could see where someone had stacked three tables on top of each other, pushed inwards slightly, the leg of the bottom table catching on the wall.

That was me, she thought, remembering how the door hadn't budged from the outside even when she kept pushing at it.

Had she scared away the people hiding in here by trying to get in? Had she forced them out into the open pool area straight into the path of the gunmen? Annie couldn't bear the guilt.

Another rustle behind the door caught Annie's breath, trapping it in her throat, squeezing her lungs. It was loud, there was something just the other side of the bamboo. She stilled, trying not to move a muscle in case it was the gunmen checking out the other rooms now all his prey were silent. He could easily slip the barrel of the gun around the door and squeeze the trigger. Slowly backing up, Annie moved away from the gap in the door and around the corner until she knew it was safe, nothing could push past the table leg propped up against the wall, Annie felt light-headed with the lack of oxygen.

The door slid closed and she gulped down a lungful of air, before it flew open as far as it would go and a tiny fluffy paw poked at the space, trying and failing to reach a dust ball trapped in the sawdust.

"What the…" Annie let out the words with her breath.

"What's happening?" Charlie called quietly from across the room. "Annie."

"It's okay. Nothing." Annie leant forwards, dropping to her knees to see better.

As the door hit the table again the paw stole back inside. It was a game to the cat. The dust ball just out of reach. In the shadows, Annie could see the cat's claws extending to long thin needles as it tried to reach its plaything.

"Shit," Annie said, wondering how the gunmen felt about animals.

It wasn't that long ago they were out on a boat with them, marvelling at the dolphins. Both Anders and Samu had relaxed then, marvelled in the playfulness of the wild animals. But a cat trapped in a hotel? Who knows? The gunman in the restaurant might shoot down a cat as quickly as he had done the man in the pool or the receptionist.

"What's going on?" Charlie made her jump, her voice right in Annie's ear.

"There's a cat," she replied, quietly.

"What? Not Cielo?"

"Don't give the bloody thing a name!" Annie hissed. "I can't leave it now, can I? Sunday would never forgive me."

"Who the hell is Sunday?"

"I don't have time to explain." Annie drew her phone out of her pocket, the screen illuminating the tiki bar like they were inside a rainbow. "Can you go and help Cielo while I call Swift? Don't open the door any further than it already is, though. If he can't squeeze through, then he'll have to fend for himself."

"He's a she," Charlie said with a huff as she tiptoed towards the tables and ducked down under them to access the door.

Annie shook her head at the young woman, secretly glad she hadn't told Annie to leave the cat alone, and dialled Swift's number.

THIRTEEN

"O'MALLEY, YOUR EARS MUST BE BURNING," SWIFT belted down the phone before Annie had a chance to speak. "I've been chasing this beast around the kitchen for the best part of three hours. He's got my phone charger, Annie. Dragging it around by the cable, he won't give it back. I've tried coaxing him out with Dreamies but he just growls at me and gives me this look. Raises one of his old man eyebrows at me. Looks at me like you do when I'm doing something stupid. Not that I'm saying you've got old man eyebrows. Yours are much shorter. In a good way. Not a shaved way. Er, anyway… is there a reason you're calling me at one in the morning?"

Annie's chest immediately expanded; it was so good to hear Swift's voice.

"10-35," she whispered, making as little noise as possible. With the windows open to the poolside, and the door banging open with the force of the cat on the other, Annie knew that her voice would carry across the air.

"Are you drunk dialling me, O'Malley?" Swift laughed and she could hear him opening the freezer and dropping ice into a glass.

The idea that Swift was safe in his kitchen, probably about to pour himself a whisky, or blend a smoothie was a double-edged sword to Annie. It was reassuring to hear him, knowing that he could help them, even if it was from a distance. But the vivid memory of his kitchen made Annie long to be there with him, chasing down the stray cat who'd stolen his phone charger, drinking whisky on a school night. Just generally doing things that didn't involve probable death.

"Swift, listen very carefully," she whispered, trying to make herself heard over the glug of liquid pouring on top of the cracking ice.

"Look, Annie, lovely," he said, jovially. "I'm going to hang up the phone because drunk dialling is never a good idea, and I don't want you to say something you'll regret."

Annie's stomach lurched. If Swift hung up, he may not answer again. It was too late to ring the office, Tink and Page would be at home asleep, and calling the UK emergency services would be confusing and not what they needed right now. There was also a dragging feeling tugging at Annie's heart, if Swift didn't want her to talk when she was drunk, he definitely didn't want to hear about the burgeoning feelings she had for him, because what else do people who drunk dial talk about? Not the weather. But Annie had stalled for long enough. Her feelings for Swift were not worth getting killed over.

"There's gunmen in the hotel, Swift," she hissed. "We need your help."

The silence on the other end of the phone was like a vacuum. Annie pulled it away from her ear to check Swift was still there.

"Swift?" she whispered, seeing the timer still increasing.

"I'm here," he said, popping the vacuum. "Talk to me."

Annie explained what had happened as succinctly as possible. Their small breakaway group, the late dinner, the shots fired, Ricky's injuries, the possible number of gunmen, no emergency services contacted. She turned away from where Charlie was trying to coax the cat inside the tiki bar and whispered about the dead bodies in the pool and reception.

"So there are five of you barricaded in the small cafe, one injured, one child?" Swift asked. Annie could hear the scratching of a pen on paper. "Remind me of the name of your hotel."

Annie reeled off the name of the luxury resort that was feeling anything but right now. "But Swift, once you've altered the authorities, I need you to check a couple of names for me."

"Annie you're not at work right now, your job is

to stay safe and stay barricaded in that room." Swift was pacing now; Annie could tell by the cadence of his voice.

"Too late, Joe," she whispered. "I'm already across the resort in the bar because there's very limited mobile coverage and the electrics are down, I needed to call for help. I needed to call you."

She felt the wobble in her throat, the stinging sensation in her nose. *Don't cry, Annie. You'll not stop.* Taking a deep breath, she went on. "There are children trapped in the main restaurant, Swift. I don't know how many are alive, and I don't want that blood on my hands. If I can work out what these men are after, then maybe I can do something to save everyone who's left alive."

"You can't tackle gunmen O'Malley," Swift replied quickly.

"I know, but I would feel a lot better if I knew what this was. Terrorists. A heist for money and jewellery. Please, Swift?"

"What are their names?"

"There are three men that we know of who are here. I only know the names of two, and only their first names. Samu and Anders. They run a chartered boat company off the dock outside the hotel. Shit, I've forgotten the name of the boat."

"Dolphin Days." Charlie was still scrambling around under the blockade of tables, but Annie heard her as clear as though she was sitting next to her.

The hum in the air had gone. Outside the window was like a pool of tar.

"The emergency back-up generator has gone off," Annie whispered to Swift after relaying the charter's name.

"They sound professional," Swift replied. "Backup generators are notoriously hard to disable. Be careful Annie."

"Always," she replied. "And Swift, please can you do a check on the hotel manifest? See if there are any guests staying here who are connected to any gangs or mafia, or any guests with unusually large bank accounts."

"Will do," he replied, still scratching the pen to paper. "Any names I can start with that you have a feeling about?"

"I don't know any of the guests," she whispered. "Just the families I'm with. Charlie and Ricky and Sofia and her son Hugo. But they're not involved, so you can cross them off and start somewhere else."

"On it," Swift said. "Now I want you to get yourself to safety, Annie. Please."

"It's pitch black out there, now," she told him. "And Charlie's rescuing a cat."

Swift let out a burst of laughter, which quickly muffled. Annie pictured him throwing a hand over his mouth to avoid undue noise. Or maybe he'd just scared Sunday further off with his charger.

"Sorry," he said. "I shouldn't laugh. But where do

you find your friends? He sounds just like you. Should I be worried?"

"Charlie's female," Annie whispered, watching as Charlie's legs shuffled back out from under the table to reveal her body, closely followed by her outstretched arms, gripping the scruff of a grey cat with huge sea blue eyes. "And she's got the cat. I'd better go."

"Call me when you can, Annie," Swift added. "What's the best way to send you info?"

"Text, please," she said. "There's only reception in this bar so that way I won't miss anything. I'll call when I can."

Swift breathed down the phone, Annie could feel the pull of words he couldn't say.

"It's okay, Joe," she said instead. "I'll be fine. I always am. And if I'm not, then Mim is a fine replacement."

She tried to get out a laugh, but it stuck in her throat like a barb. Annie knew then that she needed to get home for more than just her job and her pot plant.

Swift said a quick goodbye, promising to wake up Tink and Page and Annie slipped her phone back in her pocket and crawled to the window. Charlie was sitting with her back to the opening, cradling Cielo in her arms.

"She's fine," Charlie was saying, as the cat purred loudly.

But Annie hadn't heard the reply, not really,

because just over Charlie's head there was a movement in the darkness by the pool.

Illuminated by just the moonlight, Annie watched someone sneak up to the windows of the cafe and tug at the shutters.

"Shit," Annie muttered, watching with dread as the figure tried all the windows in turn.

There was something familiar about the movement of the person, small and slight.

"What is it?" Charlie asked, not able to move without disturbing the cat.

"Someone is out there," Annie replied.

Charlie put Cielo on the floor next to her and span around up onto her knees to look with Annie. They watched together as the figure, masked by the gloom of the broken emergency lights, went back down the cafe walls, and tried the windows again.

"They must have locked up behind us," Charlie said in Annie's ear. "Is that one of the gunmen?"

Annie shook her head. But as the figure reached up and grabbed hold of their head, pulling their hood down to reveal a high ponytail, Annie immediately recognised who it was.

"Sofia," she cried in a whisper. "She's still alive, oh thank god."

"Where has she been hiding?" Charlie added. "Thank goodness she made it. I've been so worried for poor Hugo."

"Sofia must be desperate to get back inside to see

him. She has no idea if he's okay. She must be petrified."

"Can we go to her?" Charlie was gathering Cielo up in her arms.

Annie looked between the door to the corridor and the window. If she stayed here she could contact Swift, she could listen out for the guests trapped in the restaurant, but they couldn't leave Sofia out there alone. Not now they'd seen her, not now they knew she was okay.

"Quickly," Annie said, getting to her feet. "While the emergency lights are out. Let's get down there and get you both back in the cafe."

"And Cielo?" Charlie already had the cat wrapped in her arms.

Annie nodded, she really had no choice. Not that she'd choose a different option than the one Charlie had already decided on.

"Just make sure she's wrapped up tightly in something and not likely to give us away."

Charlie slipped out of the blood stained cardigan she'd taken back from Ricky and gathered the cat up in it, tying it around her body and neck like a baby carrier. Annie wanted to laugh as the fluffy face popped out over the top of the sweater, wide eyed and curious.

"Let's go."

Annie manoeuvred her body over the window ledge and slowly let herself drop down to the sun bed below. Her bare feet made no noise and she climbed onto the tiled floor and indicated for Charlie to follow. Charlie climbed out onto the window ledge on her backside, her face twisted in panic. Behind her, Annie could hear the hammering of the door against the table inside the bar.

"Jump," she called over the noise. "Now, Charlie. Jump."

Charlie didn't wait to be told again, she dropped down from the window, one arm for balance, the other holding onto the cat in the carrier. Landing on the sun bed with a thud, Annie grabbed her arm and dragged her down and under the bar as the sound of splintering wood filled the air.

They crouched in silence, hearing the thunder of footsteps above their heads, the sound of the table scraping the floor, and the anger of the man who was doing it. In a few quick seconds he was by the window, looking out. Annie ducked her head back under and held her breath. The man hadn't seen her, but she'd seen him. Dressed all in black, a mask covering the lower half of his face, this was the man with the automatic weapon, and it was pointed in the direction of the pool.

The water lit up first, flickering like a strobe as the gunshots rang out. Empty casings clattered beside Annie and Charlie as they looked at each other, terri-fied. Charlie clung to Cielo, her nails stroking the cats head steadily and calmly. If she escaped now, there was no doubt in Annie's mind that this mad man would shoot her.

More shots rained overhead, scattering and loud. The sky lit up like fireworks and Annie had a sense of dread settling in her stomach. Sofia had been in plain slight by the cafe windows. The gunman would have seen her as soon as he fired off that first shot.

FOURTEEN

"He must have seen us," Charlie said, so quietly the words were barely a breath. "He must have heard me getting Cielo. Oh Annie, what if he's shot Sofia because I disturbed him? I couldn't live with myself if he's killed her."

Annie placed a calming hand on Charlie's bare knee and held a finger to her lips. The man had stopped firing bullets into the dark, but from the shuffling noise above their heads, Annie could tell he was still in the bar. He grunted something Spanish and threw or kicked a heavy object that battered across the floor, dropping dust down onto Annie and Charlie. Annie held her breath, not wanting the dirt to get stuck in her throat and cause her to cough. One bullet through the wooden floor could hit either of them. They had to stay as quiet as possible until the shooter had left the tiki bar.

Then what?

Annie had no idea what their plan was now. She'd gotten hold of Swift, and knew that he was calling the police, but in England they had protocols for storming a building with active shooters still present. The police here couldn't very well burst into the hotel, all guns blazing, and hope the shooter wouldn't take out more people on his way down. They would take their time surrounding the building and trying to talk to the armed men. This rescue wasn't going to be quick.

What if he got Sofia?

They needed to at least look for her. Though it would be harder now, with no emergency lighting and just the moonlight to search under, but if he'd caught Sofia with a stray bullet then Annie and Charlie could get her to safety.

Above their heads the shooter gave another angry grunt, his footsteps loud on the wood, pacing back and forth. Another clatter sounded over by the door and Annie hoped he was fighting his way out the tiki bar again, past the stacked tables. Only, moments later he jumped out the window and landed with a thud on the sun bed merely feet from Annie and Charlie.

Shit.

Annie froze, her hand still on Charlie's knee, her palms and fingers slick with sweat. Giving Charlie a very slight squeeze, the two women kept as still as possible, watching the booted feet of the shooter kick out at the sun bed. Annie thought of Ellis and Faith, and hoped with all her might that they'd stay quiet and still as the shooter stomped off in their direction.

The gun swung by his hip, the barrel visible to Annie as it pointed to the floor. Occasionally the shooter would lift it out of her view and she could picture him swinging it around, hand around the stock, finger on the trigger. Quick as a flash, a life could be over. Annie wasn't used to guns, she'd had her fair share of danger, but nothing quite so sudden and final.

The shooter worked his way down their side of the pool, kicking sun loungers and pot plants as he went. When he reached the far end of the pool and the drop off to the cliff, he turned to come back up. Annie's whole body ached with staying still. Charlie's knee was shaking under her hand, as though it was in a difficult position to hold and her muscles were about to fail. Luckily the cat seemed to have fallen asleep in the makeshift sling and was just giving the occasional snort.

The shooter's feet kicked up the dirt in the flower beds as he trampled back towards the tiki bar and carried on past them towards the reception. If he walked down the other side of the pool, there was the chance he would be able to see Annie and Charlie. They couldn't move further back, the noise and movement would give them away, no matter how dark it was. Annie just hoped that he would be so focussed on searching the area in front of him, that he wouldn't cast his eyes across the pool. She hoped even harder that he wouldn't shoot at the wooden shutters and fire directly into the cafe.

Her heart thudded loudly in her chest and her throat and her feet. The prolonged fear had made her numb, but the pain in her chest was threefold. Willing her heart not to give up on her while she was hidden in the dirt under a tiki bar, Annie watched the shooter lift his gun and aim towards the gate to the jetty and the cove. He grunted again and let off a burst of bullets into nothing but the sky, the casings clattering on the tiles beneath him.

Turning on his heels, the man stomped back to the reception area and in through the open doors. Annie couldn't see which way he went, wondering if he was looking for Anders and Samu, but knew this was their best bet for getting back inside to safety. Maybe Swift was right. Maybe she should barricade herself back in the cafe and wait for help. She had never set out trying to be a hero, and maybe this was the worst time to start.

"Can you move?" she asked Charlie.

"Yes."

"Let's go." Annie crawled out from under the bar as quietly as she could. "Back to the cafe."

Charlie nodded in the gloom and bum shuffled her way out into the open. Keeping an eye on the reception entrance, Annie ran quickly and quietly around the pool to the cafe shutters, Charlie hot on her heels. She gave the knock at the window and stood stock still, waiting for Mim to come and open them.

A cool breeze stroked at Annie's skin, prickling it with goosebumps. She felt a shiver tickle across her shoulders and tried to ignore it, any movement that wasn't necessary was a danger. The gunman might not have gone far. Anders and Samu may have been waiting for him in reception.

A flash of panic about the guests trapped in the restaurant entered her mind, but the unlocking of the shutters momentarily hushed it. Mim's face appeared at the window, puffy and red.

"We thought you'd been shot," she said, her tears glinting in the moonlight. "They sounded so close."

"One of them was out here," Annie replied, ushering Charlie to the window. "We saw Sofia."

"Is she okay?" Mim asked.

To Annie's side, Charlie was unwrapping Cielo from her cardigan, handing the sweet cat through the window to a surprised Mim.

"Hold her while I climb in," Charlie said, her hands on the window ledge. She stopped, looking down at her feet. "Annie, look."

Annie moved closer, one eye still on the reception, and looked down to see what Charlie was nodding to. Dark stains speckled the whitewash of the building. Annie looked to Charlie, her brow crumpled.

Blood.

Charlie drew her lips into her mouth as tears sprang into her eyes.

"It's okay," Annie whispered. "It's not a lot."

Annie took an unsteady breath and linked her fingers together to offer Charlie a leg up as a glut of

129

shots rang out over their heads. They dropped quickly to the floor.

"Shut it," Annie called to Mim. "Lock yourselves in, Swift's calling for help."

She wasn't sure if her sister had heard her over the shots, but there was no time to waste. Flat on the floor, belly against the cold tiles, Annie couldn't see the shooter, but she could hear him, and he was getting closer.

"With me," Annie called over the gun.

She commando crawled towards the gate as fast as she could, her elbows and stomach scraping on the rough tiles. Behind them, shots fired off into the night. The shooter, Annie wasn't sure which one it was, yelled something in Spanish with each burst of shots. Every time they clattered in the air, she winced with the fear of immediate pain, waited for the stinging sensation, or the compete blankness of death, but they never came.

They reached the gate, the gun still firing tens of shots every second, and Annie got to her knees. Glancing back, she saw the same shooter as before, his mask and hat a deep blue in the moonlight, giving him away. His gun was pointed upwards, firing into the night sky in bursts of fire and light. He wasn't looking in their direction, his face seemed to be pointed in the same direction as the rain of bullets.

"Come on," Annie called, noticing more dark drops on the tiles by the gate, a smudge of it on the post. "This way."

They ran under the cover of gunfire. Down the steep steps as fast as they dared. Annie's feet stung as she landed on the sharp stones, and it was as she was nearing the bottom of the worn steps, her foot slipped out from under her and she clattered onto the dock below. Her knee bloomed with pain; warmth spread up her leg. Charlie was right behind her, a hand out to help Annie up.

"Thanks," Annie said, wincing as she got back to her feet.

"What happened back there?" Charlie looked over her shoulder, her chest rising and falling as quickly as Annie's was. "Why is he so angry?"

Annie shrugged and shook her head, pulling her phone from her pocket to see if she had any reception and if Swift had messaged. Neither were positive outcomes.

"It feels like he's got a motive other than just shooting up a hotel," Annie said sliding her phone back, the gunfire now angry gnats in the distance. "Which might mean that the guests in the restaurant are still okay if we're lucky. Let's see if we can find Sofia."

The sea had calmed since they had disembarked from their dolphin trip and the little boat bobbed quietly on the surface.

"Inside," Annie ordered.

There were only so many places Sofia could have gone to, and if the blood on the gate was anything to go by, then Annie thought she'd headed this way too.

With the sea in front of them, and the cliff either side, it was the boat or the water. And if Sofia had been shot, the sea would have been too risky.

It was unlikely that Anders and Samu had come back this way unless they'd snuck out when Annie had been in the tiki bar. But the lights were off in the cabin, and the engine was still. Besides, they needed cover if the shooter came over to the edge of the pool again. Looking down, he'd be able to see them sitting on the dock.

They crossed the wooden dock as the gunfire stilled. It was too quiet without it, no bird noise, no cicadas, nothing. Just the sea lapping at the wooden struts and even that felt like it was too viscous to sound normal. Annie stepped down onto the bench at the back of the boat, feeling it sink into the water with her weight. She held out a hand and Charlie took it, stepping down beside her.

"Where now?" Charlie asked.

Annie felt the hairs raise on the back of her neck. They weren't alone. She could feel it in the energy around them. In the movement of the boat. There was someone else on this boat with them.

"Get behind me," Annie said, stepping carefully down onto the deck of the boat.

She crossed the floor in just a few strides, heart in her mouth. There was no sign of any blood on the white deck under her feet, there hadn't been on the wooden dock either. So Annie was almost certain it wasn't Sofia in the cabin. Annie looked around for a weapon, her eyes falling on a mini fire extinguisher. It was better than nothing. She lifted it from its hook just above the wheel.

With one hand on the cabin door, the other on the trigger of the extinguisher, Annie pulled gently and stepped into the darkness.

FIFTEEN

THE PAIN RIPPED THROUGH ANNIE'S WRIST AND radiated up her arm. She cried out, dropping the fire extinguisher with a clatter, grabbing her arm to her chest. Stepping backwards into Charlie with a grunt, Annie felt around with her good arm for the door frame to stop her falling as the door crashed closed in her face.

"Don't come in," a voice cried from the cabin. "We're armed and not afraid of you."

The voice was muffled through the wood, but Annie could hear the timbre of the words as they shook, clearly afraid.

"It's okay," Annie called back, rubbing her throbbing wrist. "We're not going to hurt you. I'm Annie and this is Charlie. We're guests at the hotel. Please let us in."

The door opened a crack and a mop of blonde hair atop huge blue eyes appeared. Annie recognised the woman from the poolside and the buffet, another guest at the hotel whose eyes widened even further when she looked at Annie and Charlie.

"Oh no," she cried, pulling the door wide and moving them inside. "I'm so sorry. Did I hurt you?"

Inside was as dark as outside, but Annie didn't need light to see that her wrist was already bruising.

"It's okay," she said, moving further into the cabin to give Charlie space behind her. "I don't blame you for hitting out. How many of you are there in here?"

She lumbered over another pair of legs and fell onto the floor. Feeling the enclosing walls around her, Annie guessed she was up near the bow of the boat.

"Four," the woman said, as a light bloomed around her from a mobile phone in her hand. "Isaac, Reuben, Kiera, and I'm Lucy."

It was a soft light from the screen of the phone, but the windows were still uncovered and one of the shooters was still at the poolside. Annie took in the collection of tired, pale looking guests sitting on the floor of the cabin around her. Two men and two women, probably around her age, dressed for dinner in dresses and trousers. Charlie had squeezed herself in between them, shivering without her cardigan. Glancing at her arm, Annie saw a bright red line across her wrist that matched the crowbar gripped in the woman's shaking hands.

"Hi. Can you turn that off, please?" Annie asked, motioning to the phone and the boat sank back into darkness. "What happened? How did you get here?"

135

"We were in the bar after dinner," one of the men started. "And we heard shouting and what we thought was fireworks. We thought someone was messing around. Firecrackers maybe, those annoying things that the kids play with back at home. But then we saw a man dressed in black burst through the hotel and shoot the guy in reception. He gave me a toothbrush... I forgot my toothbrush. And he got shot."

Annie heard the crack in the man's voice, she saw the dead body slumped by the desks and felt like crying with him.

"Sorry." He paused for a moment, clearing his throat. "Sorry. Yeah, we saw him drop; blood every-where, it was horrible. We were so scared, it's like something out of a film or a tv show. He started to move towards us, so we lifted a load of tables and barricaded ourselves in the room."

"We're not sure if he saw us," one of the women interrupted. "Because it wasn't until later that he tried to get in the bar. We heard him shouting something. One of the staff said it was something like *you can't hide from me.* Then there were more gunshots and we decided to get out the windows. We weren't safe in the bar, there's nowhere to hide if he shot down the door."

"Where are the staff who were in the bar with you?" Annie asked.

One of the women sniffed in the dark, fidgeting on the floor of the boat. It grew quiet, even the waves were muted, as if they were frightened to break the silence.

"They stayed." Annie wasn't sure which of the women had spoken. "Said they couldn't be seen to be deserting the hotel when guests needed them. The young barman spotted an older couple, I think. He was heading over to help them. We... we didn't stop to see if they were okay. We just kept running. I wanted to stop and help... but when we were halfway down the stairs, we heard shooting and..."

Her words trailed off and Annie knew instantly that the man she'd seen face down in the bloody water was the barman from the tiki bar. A sob burst up from her chest before she could stop it. In the darkness Annie felt someone's hand cover hers and squeeze it gently. It was her sore wrist, but the pain felt like a blessing of sorts, keeping her grounded, not letting her emotions topple her over the edge.

Her breath stuttered as she filled her lungs.

"You did the right thing," she said, eventually. "If you'd stayed to help, you'd all be dead. But there is some good news. The older couple, Faith and Ellis, they're okay. They found a hedge to hide in and they've been there since. I spoke to them not long ago."

Not long ago? Was it really? It felt to Annie like mere minutes had passed, but the adrenaline keeping her going was moving time around like oil on water. It wasn't linear now, it was fluid, ebbing and flowing and speeding and slowing. It might be hours since she called Swift, it might be seconds. Annie shifted her weight to the side and pulled out her phone. It was nearly two am. Almost an hour since she spoke to Joe and he promised to call for help.

"I've notified someone back home, the police, they're sorting help," she said to the group. "Did any of you see anything at all of interest about the shooters? Anything that can help identify the one with the automatic weapon?"

"Shooters?" one of the women asked. Annie thought it sounded like Lucy, the one who'd hit her with the crowbar. "There's more than one?"

"Possibly," Annie said, not wanting to alarm them anymore than they already were. "Was there anyone on the boat when you got here? Have you seen a woman, young, blond, Spanish. Possibly with a gunshot wound?"

"No," Lucy went on. "No-one. We checked first, threw stones at the windows. But it was empty. We got on and shut the door and have been hiding since. No one has been here until you both arrived. Sorry, again, about your arm."

"Lucy, you'd been shot at, I don't blame..." Annie started, until one of the men shushed her, grabbing at her arm.

He looked at her, his expression full of panic. Annie fumbled to face him as he pointed out the small porthole window. Up at the top of the steps were two figures and they were heading in the direction of the boat, fast.

Anders and Samu.

"Quick," Annie whispered at the group. "Does anyone have a knife or something sharp on them?"

Lucy answered. "I grabbed this from up top on our way into the cabin."

A blade glinted in the sliver of moonlight through the window, long and thin.

"I'm glad you opted for the crowbar when I opened the door," Annie said, trying not to imagine being shanked by the knife in Lucy's hand. She took it carefully and slid out the door. "Stay here. Do not open this door until I say it's okay."

"She's police." Annie heard Charlie say as she closed the door behind her and crept onto the deck.

Up on the steps, the shadow of the two men moved as they made their way to the boat. They were fast and mostly silent. She had to be quick if they were going to get away. Staying low, Annie moved to the stern of the boat where a thick rope tied them to the wooden dock. She slid the knife through the curve of the knot and started to saw.

The knife was sharp, but the rope was heavy and damp. The men couldn't have seen her, but Annie didn't know if she had time to cut through the rope and she had no idea how to untie the sailing knots. The knife was damp with sweat and sea spray. It slid in Annie's fingers, slipping down so the blade cut through her palm. Annie cried out at the pain, ducking lower as the shadows stopped moving in the dark.

"¡Ey!" The men called out. "¡Ey! Detener."

139

Shit.

Annie got back to her knees and sawed the knife backwards and forwards, cutting the rope as quickly as she could. Her arms screamed with the movement, her palm bleeding all over the deck and the rope and the knife. The men scrambled down the steps, stones scattering to the deck below. They were nearly there, nearly on top of them.

With a last-ditch attempt, Annie pulled the knife with all her might, dragging it through the last few cords of the rope, until it popped away and the rope splashed into the sea. Hauling herself to her feet, Annie jumped over the side of the boat and onto the dock, leaning all her weight on the hull and pushing as hard as she could. The boat was heavy at first, but as she pushed it gathered momentum and moved away from the edge.

Annie could hear the men behind her, their feet loud on the stone steps. And when the scraping turned to thuds on the wooden deck she jumped into the water, gripping tightly to the ladder at the back of the boat. Ducking underwater, Annie thought she heard the pop of gunshot and stayed there as long as her lungs would let her. Eventually surfacing, she looked back and saw that the tide and the momentum of her push was carrying them out to the entrance to the cove and the safety of the open water.

Back on dry land, the two men threw their bags to the deck and started pushing each other. Anger radiated from them, though Annie couldn't hear what they were saying or see their faces. She turned back to the boat, one hand still gripping the bottom of the ladder, and hauled herself out of the water. Shivering and dripping with water, she stumbled back to the cabin door and knocked.

"It's me," she called. "Does anyone know how to hot wire a boat?"

Lucy pushed the door open and threw an arm around Annie.

"Look for towels and something dry." She drew Annie inside the cabin, moving her out of the way of one of the men heading topside, and shut the door. "Check the cupboards, check everywhere."

"You'll be getting a reputation as being bossy," Annie joked, her teeth clattering together with the cold. "Take it from someone who's been there."

"Sit down," Lucy ordered as the other man wrapped a zip up hoody over Annie's shoulders and Charlie started bandaging her palm with a ripped up towel. "At least all your injuries are on the same arm."

A bubble of laughter popped from Annie's throat as she looked at her bruised, swollen, bleeding arm. She'd take that as a win too. Above their head the boat stuttered into life, the random bobbing in the waves stopped as they moved forwards with speed.

"I hope he knows what he's doing," Charlie said, as they took a corner fast enough to topple them all sideways.

Lucy climbed over Annie and sat down next to her.

"Are we safe now?" she asked, a sob racking through her body. "Annie? Are we okay?"

"What about Ricky?" Charlie asked quietly, hands paused on Annie's dressing.

Annie's stomach clenched like a fist, her muscles shook, her whole body burned as she realised that they may be safe now, but they were heading away from the hotel and from Mim and Hugo and Ricky.

"I'm not giving up on them," Annie said, clasping her hands around Charlie's. "We're not giving up on them."

She looked out the window as they rounded the bay and could see nothing of their hotel, as though it was no longer there. On either side, lights blazed, and pools lit up the night sky as the other hotels carried on as though nothing was wrong.

SIXTEEN

"Does anyone know how to park a boat?" A voice shouted through the cabin doors. "If so, please make yourself known because we're... eek."

The boat juddered, thumping against something, and throwing the women onto each other. Both the men were up top, supposedly steering the boat around the bay and directly to the nearest dock so they could all disembark and call for local help. An ear-piercing screech of metal on metal sounded along the side of the hull and made Annie's teeth crawl.

"I hope we're near land," she said, unravelling her arms and legs from around Charlie's. "Because that sounds like it might have done more damage than an iceberg and I don't fancy swimming in these waters in the dark."

Shuddering as she remembered Anders telling her about the sharks, Annie pulled open the door to the cabin and stepped out into the night.

Anders.

He'd seemed so kind and generous, not to mention gorgeous. Annie still couldn't picture that man as a stone-cold killer. Samu, more so, but Anders seemed genuinely a nice person. But she'd seen Samu and Anders in the hotel with a gun. People were dead. It wrote itself, really.

Isaac and Reuben were studying the wheel, both with a tight grip on the rubber. They'd steered them straight at the dock and a metal ladder leading up to the high wooden jetty was stuck fast in the carbon of the side of the hull.

"We were going a bit fast," The brown haired one said, Annie still wasn't sure which was Isaac and which was Reuben.

"You think?" she replied, eyebrows raised. She went over to assess the damage. "Turn off the engine if you can. No idea how that works when you hot wire a boat."

The engine clicked off, ticking in the night as it cooled. Water lapped at the boat, and in the distance the sound of music and parties cut through the night, incongruous to the disaster they'd left behind.

"The keys were in the ignition."

What?

Annie could feel the cogs turning in her mind. Something was brewing there; she just wasn't sure what yet. Clearing her head, she looked down to where the ladder had scraped the hull. The paintwork was no longer, and there were two large gouges in the fibreglass. She leant as far as she could over the side, noting that the ladder only went as far as a few inches under the water level.

"I think she'll be okay," Annie said, facing the two men. "There's no sign that the breakage is all the way through."

The blond man shrugged. "Doesn't matter though, does it, Reuben?" He looked to his friend. "We're getting off here. We're not going back."

Annie nodded. "Gather your stuff, get to the nearest hotel, and tell them what's happening. Tell them to call the police. Unless…"

Annie pulled her phone from her pocket, hearing the three women climb out of the cabin and onto the deck. Their low chatter was sluggish and resigned, their adrenaline depleted, leaving them husks of skin and bone. She held the phone to her face and the screen lit up, dotted with notifications and messages from Swift with three whole bars of reception.

"Charlie," Annie said, sitting on the bench at the back of the boat, eyes not leaving her phone. "Get out with these guys and stay safe."

Annie swiped at the screen and read:

> Called the police. They're on their
> way. Stay safe, O'Malley.

Tink and Page are on it. We're at the office searching hotel manifest and the names you gave me. Anders. Samu. Charlie and Ricky. Sofia and Hugo.

Tink says why can't you just have a normal holiday like a normal person?

Scrap that, she says I wasn't supposed to ask you. Rhetorical question.

I hope you're okay, Annie.

Police called. They're surrounding the building, but they can't enter until they know more about the gunman. Active shooter means they can't storm.

Annie, message when you can, I'm worried about you.

O'Malley, if you're reading this, I want you to know that if you don't make it home, I'm turning Sunday into a rug.

Annie, if you don't make it home, I'm going to kill you myself.

Please call me. I don't want to be without you.

Annie felt her stomach flip. He'd sent the last message a few minutes ago. She swiped some more and tapped dial, but Charlie took her phone from her hands and ended the call before it connected.

"What, give me that back, Charlie," Annie cried, standing, and grabbing out at the young woman's hands. "Now. I need to call Swift."

"I'm not leaving this boat until you do, Annie." Charlie took a step back, moving Annie's phone out of reach. "You can't order me to leave and go somewhere safe, until you tell me what your plans are."

Annie didn't have time for this. "Give me my phone back." Over Charlie's shoulder, Annie saw the four of the escapees watching on as the girls argued. "You're putting everyone at danger, Charlie. I'm going back to try and get Mim and Ricky and Hugo on the boat, to bring them and anyone else I can to safety. Ellis and Faith have been out in the cold for too long, they're in danger."

"But if you go back, you're in danger too," Charlie shouted. "The gunmen are still there. They'll hear the boat. You don't even know how to drive a boat."

Annie sighed, Charlie was right, but it was too far to go back to the hotel on land, and that's if they could even get a car. It was around the bay, much further by the winding roads, and when they got there, the door would be locked, and it was too hard to break in through the front. That's why the gunmen had taken the boat in the first place. Another thought

147

niggled at Annie's brain, and she stored it away for later.

"But what choice do I have?" Annie asked. "My sister is still there. That young boy, Hugo, who was so scared. Ricky and probably Sofia are bleeding out. If I don't go, and something happens to them, I will never forgive myself. Please, Charlie. Just get out of the boat and go and get help."

Lucy approached, tentatively, wrapping an arm around Charlie's shoulder.

"Come on," she said, gently. "Give Annie her phone back and we'll get somewhere warm and dry. You look like you could use a drink and some clean clothes."

Charlie looked down at her blood-stained shorts and thin vest-top, her arms pink where Ricky's blood had dried onto her skin when it seeped through her cardigan. With red eyes she looked back at Annie, passing her the phone.

"Please be careful," she said, going with Lucy and the others. "And look after Ricky for me."

Annie nodded, feeling the sway of the boat as they climbed one by one up the ladder to the jetty and safety. The pull of longing was strong, she wanted to go after them, to head up the ladder and into a warm, dry hotel with tea making facilities and no trigger-happy gunmen waiting to shoot them down.

"Urgh." Annie swiped her phone open and called Swift.

"Oh my god, O'Malley," Swift said, answering

almost immediately. "You're okay. You are okay, aren't you? This is you and not some policeman calling to tell me the bad news? Are you a policeman? Do you speak English?"

"It's me, Swift," Annie burst out. "It's me. I'm safe for the moment."

"Ohthankgod." The words came out as one long breath. "Annie I was so worried."

"Tell me what you know," she replied, having wasted enough time arguing with Charlie.

Swift barked out a laugh. "Forever in work mode."

"I wasn't," Annie acquiesced a little softer. "I was sunbathing in my smallest bikini with a drink in each hand. But needs must, hey?"

"Christ." Swift cleared his throat. "Totally put me off my stride there, O'Malley. Right, hold on, let me put you on speakerphone so Tink and Page can hear you too. I'm assuming you're somewhere you can talk?"

"I'm on a boat," Annie replied, hauling herself over to the wheel and turning the key. Charlie had been right, Annie had no idea how to drive a boat, but it surely couldn't be that different to a car. Could it? "I'm at a dock a little over from the hotel. But I'm heading back in."

"Right." Annie loved Swift for not arguing with her, she knew he'd go back for Mim and the others too. A couple of beeps sounded out on the phone and

Annie heard the comforting voices of her other teammates.

"Annie, only you, hey?" It was good to hear Page.

"Hi Page," Annie replied. "Hi Tink."

"Annie," Tink shouted. "We've got info, are you ready to hear it?"

Annie drew the throttle back and the boat listed to the side, still stuck on the bars of the ladder.

"Give me two minutes," she called back, hitting speaker on her own phone and laying it on the wheel. "I've just got to get the boat moving."

Jumping over a pile of life jackets, Annie moved to the side of the boat and pushed the ladder, wincing as the metal creaked and groaned on the plastic. The water splashed up at her between the boat and the ladder, soaking the sleeves of the hoody she'd stolen. Pulling her sleeves up, Annie gave a great shove against the ladder, pain rippling through her hand and her arm, and the boat broke free sending her flying onto the side and almost headfirst into the water. She let out a cry, grabbing out with her hands for anything she could get a hold of, and wrapping her fingers into the foam of the bench.

"You okay, Annie?" Came the tinny voice of Swift from her phone.

"Yeah," she shouted back, hoping he could hear her. "Just a minute."

Letting her body balance itself, Annie pushed herself back upright and skipped over the life jackets and back to the wheel.

"Right," she said, popping the throttle in reverse and moving the boat away from the jetty. In front of her, Charlie and the others were nowhere to be seen, behind was a vast expanse of dark water. Annie felt scared, but she pushed through it and guided the boat around until she was facing the cliffs and the bay beyond. "I'm here. Talk to me."

"Tink?" Swift said, and Tink's voice came over the speaker.

"Annie, like Swift said, the police are currently surrounding the building, but they need more information before they can go in. And information is my middle name."

Annie heard Page over the speaker. "I thought your middle name was Rhinehart?"

"I'm sorry, what?" She couldn't let this one slide. "Rhinehart?"

"Shut up, both of you," Tink replied. "And I told you that in secret, Thomas! Annie, ignore him, he's a dick. Anyway, back to your hotel. We searched the manifest, there's nothing in it to raise concerns about any of the guests or any of the staff."

"Oh no," Annie gasped. "That means it's terrorists, right? That means that no matter what I do to try and negotiate, there is no negotiating."

"You're not negotiating with anyone, O'Malley,' Swift called, his voice sounded echoey, as though he was standing away from the phone.

"He's right," Tink added. "And please don't even try, Swift has been pacing like a trapped animal since you called. It's doing my head in. But we don't think it is terrorists, Annie. For a start, no one group has claimed responsibility, in fact it's very quiet on the net so far, nothing written anywhere about what's happening. And get this. We searched Samu and Anders, and what we found is weird. Anders has owned Dolphin Days for at least three years, but Samu isn't on the register. Samu is a carpenter by trade from what we could find."

"That's weird." Annie slowed the throttle and edged the boat out into the open sea, turning towards the blackness of her hotel.

"That's not the weirdest thing, though," Tink added. "We dug into Samu's family, which was hard, took a lot of digging to find because his social media is tighter than Swift's wallet. But get this, Samu has a sister and a nephew staying at the hotel. Two of the people hiding in the cafe with you. Sofia and Hugo. Samu is Sofia's brother."

SEVENTEEN

"SAMU IS SOFIA'S BROTHER? BUT THAT MAKES NO sense," Annie said. "They barely acknowledged each other today, yesterday, whenever it was we went on our dolphin watching boat trip. And surely a small child is going to be super excited to see his uncle?"

"I don't know the answer to that one, O'Malley." Swift was on the line now. "Can you ask Sofia?"

An image flashed before Annie's eyes. Sofia trying the cafe shutters. The gunman firing into the darkness towards her.

"I don't know where she is, Swift," she replied. "I think she's hurt. She was shot at, not by Samu or Anders, but by the other guy. How is she involved?"

"We're working on the answer to that. What's your plan now?"

"I'm heading back to the hotel as we speak," Annie said, steering the boat as carefully as she could through the entrance to the hotel cove.

The cliffs encroached on either side, and Annie didn't know how far out they came under the water. If she scraped a hole in the boat or became stuck on hidden rocks, Annie didn't fancy her chances in the water. Over the edge, it was like tar, black and impenetrable, the surface waves choppy and rough. Annie knew how cold it was and how far away from the dock she was. Pulling the throttle to an almost standstill, Annie guided the boat as slowly as possible through the gap in the cliffs.

"And then what?" Swift asked, reminding her the team were there with her.

"Then I thought I might have a margarita and a dip in the pool," she snapped back. "I have no idea, Swift. Literally none."

"It's okay, O'Malley," Swift replied. "Let me help you. You're not alone."

Out in the middle of the Mediterranean, Annie felt very much alone.

"Sorry," she muttered. "I'm scared, Swift. Really scared."

"I know," Swift replied. "And that's okay. Use that fear to make you work well. Some of your best calls have been made when you're scared. No one in their right mind would have rescued Sunday without a side order of panic."

Annie couldn't help but laugh. "Nice deflection, Joe," she said softly.

"The police are trying to work out a line of communication with the gunmen. I've passed on the details of Samu and Anders to them. We don't know the third perp, as of yet, but two is good to start." Swift had switched to work mode. "They're going to try and infiltrate from the sea. I passed on what I could garner from our conversation, and they know the cove well. But anything else you can think of that might be useful?"

Annie wracked her brain for her memory store of information. It was hard, wading through the panic and fear to find titbits that might be of use. It was like waking from a dream and trying to remember what happened, and the more she tried, the harder it was.

"The gate was broken," she said, eventually, a lightbulb moment. "The gate from the pool side to the cove. It's the only access to the hotel that isn't key carded or electronic. It was broken last night. Or it could have been the night before last. Whatever day it was, it was jimmied open by a child's spade."

"Good work, O'Malley," Swift said. "From the inside or out?"

Annie's blood ran as cold as the water under the boat. Her skin broke out in goose flesh, ripe and fierce.

"The inside," she whispered, kicking herself that she hadn't realised the significance of this before. "Swift..."

"I know what you're thinking Annie," he said.

"That's more than me," Annie interrupted. "I'm nearly back to the dock. I need to turn the engine off and stay quiet."

"Okay," Swift replied. "There's one thing you should be aware of. If you can, get to the lowest point of the hotel, there's a boiler room beneath the reception area, the door is just under the stairs. The boiler room has one exit and entrance, it's windowless and easy to barricade yourselves in. I'll tell the police to look there for survivors. If you can't get everyone back to the boat to escape, that should be your next option. If it's safe to move at all."

"Thanks Swift," Annie said, killing the engine and lifting her phone to her ear, switching it off speaker. "Thank you. I'm sorry for getting you embroiled in this, but I didn't know who else to call."

"Never apologise for asking me for help, Annie." Without speaker phone, it sounded as though Swift was standing next to her.

Annie felt a sob grow in her throat and tried to swallow it down. Taking a deep breath before she could continue.

"I'm here," she whispered back.

"Be careful, Annie. I…" Swift couldn't finish his sentence; Annie could hear the crack in his words and the fizzle of the reception cutting out.

"I know, Swift," she finished for him. "I know."

She hung up the phone and slid it back into her pocket, waiting as the boat glided through the water, propelled on by the residual momentum. The dock looked empty, thankfully, because the boat was gliding towards it with a speed that Annie couldn't control. She turned the wheel, letting the already damaged side take the brunt of the collision, and held on for dear life as the boat listed precariously into the dock. As it righted itself, Annie let go of the wheel and scrambled across the slippery floor.

Grabbing one of the life jackets, Annie tied the cord around the metal railing on the boat and hooped the sleeve over the wooden strut on the dock. Hoping it would hold, she slipped out of the boat and started back up the steps to the gate.

The hotel was quiet. No gunshots, no crying. Just the peaceful chirp of the cicada and the croak of the occasional frog. Annie snuck back through the broken gate, checking the lock again. It was definitely broken from the inside, the bent metal only accessible from the pool area when the gate was shut.

She snuck around the pool, listening out for footsteps and gunshots. But there was nothing.

"Hello," she whispered, heading to the hedge. "Faith, Ellis?"

"The bush rustled and Ellis stuck a hand out. "Still here, young lady."

"There's a room under the reception. The boiler room. It's safer there, and warm." Annie didn't waste any time with niceties. "Do you think you can get to it? The door is just under the stairs behind the reception desk. Go, while it's still dark. As soon as the sun comes up, you'll be too visible."

She took Faith's hand and helped her up, hearing the crunch of the older woman's knees as they straightened and locked.

157

"Thank you," Faith whispered. "It's getting cold out here."

"Any signs of the shooters since I've been gone?" Annie asked, helping Ellis up next. He tried hard not to groan, but it escaped his lips as he stood.

"There was a young woman over there," Ellis said, nodding to the cafe window. "She was hit, I don't know where she went but she didn't look good."

Annie felt sick. "Sofia," she whispered. "Thanks Ellis. Go. Now. Lock the door if you can. I'm going to get some others and meet you down there. I'll knock a *shave and a haircut* when we get there, if you could please let us in. The police are on their way and if we can stay hidden in the boiler room there's a chance we'll be okay."

Annie walked around the pool with the old couple, trying not to hurry them, but their steps were unsteady and frustratingly slow.

"Don't look behind the desks," Annie whispered, ushering them inside. "Get to the door and go straight down."

She watched as the couple disappeared into the darkness of the reception then spun on her heels and ran across the tiles to the cafe. Knocking on the cafe window, Annie didn't have to wait long before Mim's face appeared again.

"Annie," she hissed, practically hauling her by the hood through the window. "You're putting the fear of god into me every time you leave."

Annie dropped to the floor, catching her breath as

Mim locked up the shutters behind her. Plunged into darkness, Annie took a moment to readjust her eyes. She felt Mim's breath on her face, her hands wrapping around her own.

"What happened?" Mim asked. "Where's Charlie?"

They sat for a while, as Annie told Mim what had happened after they'd unceremoniously dumped the cat on Mim. The boat, the others going for help, the boiler room.

"And you came back?" Mim said, and Annie could hear the tears thick in her throat.

"Of course I came back," she replied, squeezing Mim's hand. "How's Ricky? Where's Hugo?"

Mim got to her feet, pulling Annie up behind her, and walked over to the tables. They ducked down and looked at Ricky, paler than Annie thought a human could get, his chest barely moving. And Hugo, sound asleep on the floor, his arms wrapped around Cielo.

"There's no way we can move him," Mim said. "I've been trying to get him sips of water, but he's just sleeping now. He's barely awake."

"We need to move him," Annie said, looking around for something they could use as a stretcher. "He's not safe here. None of us are."

"Do you know what the gunmen are after? What did Swift say?"

Annie's eyes settled on the trestle table blocking the door. If they could get Ricky on there, it was long enough to carry him with.

"There's no obvious reason for the attack," Annie whispered, moving to the table and lifting off the fruit and the water. "But Swift isn't sure it's terrorist related because no one is claiming it's them, he thinks it's targeted."

"Targeted to what? Who?" Mim was beside her, helping.

"We don't know, yet. But I think it's got something to do with Sofia." Annie didn't want to admit it, but it was too much of a coincidence for one of the shooters to be connected to a guest and that not to have something to do with the siege.

"What?" Mim stopped what she was doing, a bunch of bananas in her hands. "Why?"

Annie looked under the table, double checking that Hugo was asleep. "Because Samu is her brother."

Mim was as shocked as Annie had been. Something flashed in her eyes, anger maybe, hurt.

"What do you think?" Mim asked, laying the bananas on the floor and lifting the table on Annie's command.

"I think maybe it's an inside job." Annie nodded to Mim to put the table gently by their hiding spot. "Sofia broke the gate and let her brother and the other men in. Maybe they're thieves, maybe it's more sinister than that. Sofia could have been casing the place since she's been here. The dolphin trip was a ploy to get the boat here."

"What's her motive?" Mim asked.

"That's a missing puzzle piece," Annie replied,

chewing her lip. "Whatever it is Sofia is after, I think it went wrong. Because when Charlie and I were in the tiki bar, the gunman shot right at her."

"Double crossed?"

"Maybe." Annie squatted back down to assess the situation. "Or maybe she'd served her purpose, and that gunman is a ruthless as she is."

"We need to find out what's special about this hotel."

"No, we need to get you all to safety," Annie interrupted, ignoring Mim's narrow eyes and shuffling around behind Ricky. "Here, give me a hand, you grab his legs and I'll get his head."

EIGHTEEN

"No me dejes," Hugo looked up at Annie with wide eyes and a trembling lip.

He scrambled out from under the shelter of the table, gripping the makeshift stretcher table until his fingers turned white. Annie looked to Mim and back to the young boy. He looked like a wreck, a hollowed-out shell of the boy who'd leapt into the pool and swam carefree and wild only hours ago.

Bending down to his eye level, Annie peeled his hand away from Ricky and held them in her own. His palms were slick with sweat.

"You're safe here," she said, hating herself for lying, but they couldn't carry Ricky and Hugo. "We'll come right back for you."

"Quiero a mi mami," he said, and Annie recognised the word for mummy and felt her heart lurch. "¿Dónde está mi papá?"

"Maybe he should just come with us now?" Mim

said, wiping her forehead with her arm, her short hair sticking up away from her eyes.

"What if they're out there?" Annie had gone over this in her head as she'd formulated the plan. If they took Ricky to safety, they had no way of protecting Hugo while they were carrying the table. If the gunman was out there, Annie knew Mim and she could run and hide. Yes, they'd have to leave Ricky, but she couldn't risk it with Hugo. Not with someone so young. "I'll come back for him as soon as you and Ricky are downstairs."

Mim looked at Hugo who'd dropped to his knees and wrapped his arms tightly around Annie. "What if you take Hugo first?

"Because if they're out there, he stands no chance," Annie whispered, not giving away the meaning of her words with the tone of her voice, thankful for once that Hugo had no idea what she was saying. "At least if we go first, I can check the coast is clear."

"So go do that now," Mim said, looking towards the unblocked door.

"Mim, please. I've thought this through. I'm not saying this lightly and out of lack of compassion. The more times we're out there, the more danger we're in. Please, let's just take Ricky and I'll come straight back for Hugo."

She turned back to the young boy, stroking his fingers.

"You've got Cielo," she said, glancing around the room for the cat. "She'll protect you."

Cielo was still under the table, curled in a ball sleeping. Oblivious to the danger, a soft purr emanated from her fluff like a steam engine. Annie extracted an arm from Hugo's grip and made kissy noises at the cat until it lifted its head and opened an eye.

"Cielo," Annie whispered. "Look Hugo."

Hugo looked at Cielo and sighed. Letting go of Annie, he stood, but instead of crawling back under the table, he stepped across to Mim and grabbed at her leg.

"This isn't right," Mim said, shuffling her feet, her hand on Hugo's head. "I don't want to leave without him."

Annie's stomach churned. Either way they were all putting themselves in danger, but if Mim wasn't going to leave without the boy then Annie had no other option.

"Okay." She nodded, but you need to keep him close to your side. "Wait here."

Annie swore beneath her breath and went to check the hallway. Pulling open the door, she looked out into the gloom. Outside, the sun was starting to rise, spreading light through the windows in small squares across the hallway floor. There was no one out there. Annie closed her eyes and held her breath. There was no noise out there either.

"Ready?" She looked back at her sister.

"Ready." Mim nodded.

Annie walked back and took her end of the table. Ricky's eyes hadn't opened since they moved him, a slow trickle of blood seeped from the wound on his side on to the top of the table, pooling around Annie's old cardigan.

"Okay," she said. "On three. One, two…"

"Gata, gata," Hugo cried, dropping back to his knees, and hurrying under the table.

Cielo gave a rumble of annoyance as he dragged her out with her back legs and gathered her up into his arms. A thought flashed across Annie's mind of her trying to do that to Sunday and probably losing an eyeball or two. Hugo gathered the cat into his arms and poked a hand free from the fur to grab hold of Mim's leg.

"Three?" Annie raised her eyebrows in question at Mim and they lifted together.

The table was heavy enough without the weight of Ricky. With the injured man, Annie felt her arms struggle to keep it off the floor. Mim's face pinkened with the exertion too, but her jaw was set and firm. Annie walked backwards out of the door, taking it slow and steady, trying not to trip over her own feet or the legs of the table. Ricky wobbled precariously, his arms hanging off the sides.

"Watch the vase," Mim whispered, looking past Annie.

Annie glanced over her shoulder and spotted the sideboard with the apples and water and the frippery that seemed out of place now, and side stepped to avoid it.

Ricky let out a groan, shifting his weight on the table, his arms splaying further. Annie gripped tighter, feeling the wood slipping from her fingers, trying to right the angle it had moved to but overshooting it and almost throwing Ricky over the other side. Mim's face scrunched, her arms were shaking.

"Put him down," Annie said, but Mim shook her head as Ricky moved again, his arms jerking to the sides as he felt the impetus of downward movement.

Even in a state of shock the body can feel when it's falling, and Ricky's reactions were working over-time to stop it happening. As his body twitched and his arms froze, his hands hit out at the sideboard knocking into the vase and sending it spinning around on its base. The two women watched on in horror as it toppled, spinning around and around, getting lower. The noise of the ceramic on the wood was as loud as a gong, echoing down the corridor and alerting everyone to their presence.

The vase rattled and settled on its side, rolling toward the edge and the tiled floor beneath it. If it fell and smashed, it was game over. Annie watched, unable to move, her legs stuck to the floor, her arms still holding up the makeshift stretcher.

"Mim," she whispered, feeling completely out of control.

And as the vase dropped to the floor and Annie's stomach went with it, Hugo darted out from under

Mim's legs and caught it on the fluffy body of Cielo. The young boy's lips curled. Though his eyes looked hollowed and drawn, Annie was relieved to see him smiling.

"Good job, Hugo," she whispered. "Good job."

She had no idea if he knew what she was saying, but the smile stayed on his face as he propped the vase back up and curled back around Mim's legs.

Somewhere in the distance a door clicked shut. The adrenaline pumped around Annie's body, propelling her out of the inertia and back into action.

"Move," she cried, and started walking towards the reception and the door to the boiler room.

Her arms were shaking, lactic acid pumping through them, her injured palm stinging, but they couldn't stop now. The reception was aglow with the oranges and reds of the sunrise, blood splatter clear as day on the desktop and the wall behind it. Bile rose in Annie's throat, and she tried to swallow it down, the stench of metal clinging to her nose and mouth.

"Don't look," she said, wishing she could protect Hugo from the sight. "Just keep walking."

But Hugo was scared. He stopped moving, eyes wide and fixed on the blood. Mim stumbled over him where he was tangled in her legs and knocked him sideways, Cielo falling from his arms. Hugo didn't even flinch as the cat landed on her feet and trotted towards the reception desks. He was in shock, his legs trembled and his face grey.

"Quick," Annie called to Mim, still carrying the table around the reception desks to the stairs. "Move."

They dragged Ricky across the reception, manoeuvring past the desks and the dead body hidden behind them, until they reached the stairs and the hidden door to the basement. It was barely visible, the seams blending into the stairs and the handle a simple finger hole. Annie put her end of the table down, silently begging Ricky not to roll or move again. She slid her finger into the door and tugged at it. It was locked.

Ellis and Faith.

She stepped back, knocking as lightly as she could to alert the older couple.

"Come on, come on."

Annie knocked again a little harder, the sound of footsteps circled around above their heads.

"Go get Hugo," Annie whispered to Mim, who was staring up the stairs at the noise. "Now."

Mim didn't need telling twice. She ran back to the boy and scooped him up in her arms. He looked like a deadweight, the way his legs dangled, and his hands fell flat.

The footsteps were getting louder. Annie knocked again, one last time before they had to run and leave Ricky. And this time the door clicked and opened slightly.

"It's me," Annie said, pushing her fingers in the gap in the door and pulling it open.

Ellis stood beyond, frail and shivering in the stairwell.

"Can you help?" she asked him.

Immediately he moved forward, grabbing Hugo from Mim's arms and hushing him like he was his own grandchild. They disappeared down the stairs into the darkness.

Mim had already managed to get her arms under Ricky's shoulders and was trying to lift him from the makeshift stretcher. Annie grabbed his legs and together they half lifted half dragged him through the doorway. Ellis was halfway back up the stairs when Annie heard the shouts.

"Take him," she called to the older man, shifting out of the way so she could pass over Ricky's legs.

"Annie," Mim hissed. "What are you doing?"

"I need to distract them," she cried. "I can't let them see where you're all going."

And as Annie ran to the top of the stairs, a flash of red t-shirt flew past her and out the door at the top.

"Cielo," Hugo called, his arms flailing. "Cielo. Mama."

Annie couldn't stop him in time. She didn't see it was the young boy until it was too late. He stumbled at the door, picking himself up and hurtling back out into the reception. Annie ran after him, slamming the hidden door shut behind her to try and protect her sister and the others.

"Hugo," Annie called after him as quietly as she

could, but he was too fast as he took off out of reception and headed for the pool. "Stop. Shit."

It was as though Hugo saw the floating body at the same moment Annie remembered it was there. Now the sun was starting to shine, Annie could see the white shirt and black trousers of the staff uniform. The barman was still face down, but the water was pink and bubbling around it.

Hugo let out a blood curdling scream and fell backwards.

Running out into the rising sun to try and help, Annie rounded the desks straight into the hard chest of Samu.

NINETEEN

ANNIE COULDN'T WORK OUT IF SHE WAS ALIVE OR dead. Her heart wasn't beating, her mouth was dry, her limbs felt numb and detached.

Time had slowed as she'd run full force into the grumpy man from the boat who'd been brandishing a gun. And now it was catching up with a dizzying whirr of sound and a flash of light. Beyond Samu, Hugo was curled in a ball on the tiled ground, rocking back and forth, whimpering like a puppy for his mamá. Something in Annie stirred. She felt rage bubble up from the bottom of her stomach.

How dare you, she thought, *he's just a child.*

Samu stared at her, stunned almost as much as Annie had been. He lifted his arms, and she knew she had to act before he shot her. Groping around behind her, Annie's fingers brushed something cool and hard.

The vase.

She wrapped her fingers around the neck and

hurled her arms towards Samu, striking him in the side of the head. He cried out as the ceramic smashed across his skull, scattering in tiny pieces over the tiles and sticking in his thick hair like confetti.

"Que..." he cried out, hands flying to his head, fingers coming away red with blood.

Annie ran. Not waiting to see how hurt Samu was, she took her chance and flew past him and out into the pool area. Grabbing Hugo's arm, Annie lifted him off the floor and into her arms, hugging him closely. She took off again, stumbling over a broken plant pot and almost dropping to her knees. She daren't look back, she could feel the breath of Samu on her neck as she ran around the pool and hopped back onto the sun lounger under the window of the tiki bar.

Arms screaming, Annie lifted Hugo as high as she could, until he gripped the window ledge and hurled himself inside. Annie jumped as high as she could, the sun lounger skidding out from under her feet. Her fingers caught the edge of the window but couldn't find purchase. She tumbled to the tiles, her ankle turning with a jolt of pain that twisted up through her leg and juddered in her hip.

Annie cried out, hopping in a circle to find the sun bed and drag it back into position. Glancing up at the reception, Samu was brushing the debris from his thick hair. He was quiet though, Annie thought he'd be calling for backup and felt relieved he wasn't. Maybe she'd stunned him more than she realised.

Wasting no more time, Annie hauled herself back

to the sun bed and threw herself as high as she could, grunting with the effort. Her fingers brushed the windowsill and with the last ounce of strength left in her arms, she gripped on as tightly as she could. It wasn't enough, she could feel her hands slipping, sweat making her palms slick, she couldn't get purchase.

Samu called out from behind her.

Swift, Annie called in her head, *please help me.*

There had been times in Annie's past where she had felt on the edge of something that could end it all. Those times had been painful. Those times had been the most scared Annie had felt. But in all those moments where she feared for her life, there had been one constant. Swift.

But now he was thousands of miles away and wasn't going to burst through the door to save her at the last minute. He wasn't her knight in shining armour. He couldn't help her.

Annie are you mental? His voice sounded out in her head. *You don't need me to save you.* You *found those missing girls.* You *fought the crazy schoolgirl hell bent on finishing anyone who dared look at her boyfriend.* You *stopped the plague doctor in his tracks, not me. Not me. None of it was me. I'm barely more use than Tink's keyboard. Don't call out to me for help when all this time you've managed by your-self.* All this time. *Growing up it was always you.*

Annie let out a roar, the fear in her throat thrown out by the power she felt. Swift was right. *She* was

173

right. Annie didn't need anyone else to save her, she could do it herself. Pulling with all her might, arms pulsing with pain, she lifted her body up to the window ledge and dragged herself through. Kicking out, Annie dropped over into the tiki bar, panting and exhausted.

Annie struggled up, her ankle swollen, her sore arm pulsing, her whole body screaming at her to just let it rest. But she couldn't. Not when Samu would have seen where she had gone.

In the light of the morning, the bar looked as broken as Annie felt. Table were upended, broken glass glistened on the floor. In the corner, huddled against the world, was Hugo. She ran to him, gathering him up in her arms again and pushing on to the door. Moving Hugo around to her hip, Annie used her free arm to lift the tables out of the way and open the door just wide enough for them to escape the bar. She ran down the steps to the corridor, glancing back and forth. Both sides were clear, but she didn't know where to go. Right to reception and the possibility of safety in the basement. But Samu was there, and Annie didn't want to run into him again. Left to the restaurant and the other guests being held hostage by the third gunman.

The cupboard.

Annie took a left, bursting across the tiled floor and around the corner to the restaurant door and the small corridor to the cleaner's cupboard. Angry shouts echoed around the corridor. They were Spanish, nearby, and followed up with a guttering punch of bullets. Annie's blood curdled, and she pulled open the door to the cupboard with such force that it banged against the wall behind it. She hoped the noise would be drowned out by the gunfire as she ducked inside and dropped to her knees.

Plunged into darkness as the door swung shut, Hugo held onto her neck, not willing to let go.

"Hush, little one," Annie whispered, stroking his hair, and trying to peel his arms away from her windpipe so she could breathe. "It's okay. We're safe now, we're safe."

She felt him tremble in her arms and held him close until his breathing relaxed and the warmth returned to his fingers. Outside the safety of the cupboard a door rattled and slammed shut.

"Mamá," Hugo called out, and Annie hushed him as best she could, her eyes squeezed tightly shut.

Mamá. She hadn't seen Sofia since she'd been shot at out by the poolside. It didn't bear thinking about what might have happened to her since then. Annie hoped the young mother had found a place to hide just like her son was now.

"We'll find her." Annie rocked Hugo as she spoke. "I'll do everything I can to find her, Hugo. I promise."

Through the darkness of the cupboard Annie heard a howling that cut through her senses like a knife. She was glad Hugo couldn't see her face as her eyes filled with tears. The gunman was stepping it up a notch, his anger had switched to something more visceral. The fear wrenching through Annie was poker hot.

Hugo gripped tighter, Annie whispered in his ear, trying to fend off the attack of screams from outside the door.

A door rattled again in the corridor and the screams got louder. But when the gunman stopped his keening and an eerie silence fell over them, Annie wanted it back. Anything back. She couldn't stand the quiet that bloomed against her ears and made her feel like she was drowning. At least when the gunman was shouting, Annie could tell where he was. Now he could be anywhere. He could be right outside the cupboard.

"Por favor. No es justo. Dónde estás." The gunman was muttering. His footsteps marching back and forth not far from their hiding place.

Annie didn't know what he was saying. Though she understood *please*. What could he be pleading for? A man who'd coldly shot down two members of staff and goodness knows how many guests was pleading for what? Forgiveness? Probably not.

Hugo shuffled under her arms, pushing his way out of her hold.

"Qué?" The young boy stuck his neck out, listening to the gunman as his muttering continued in the corridor.

He sounded like a madman, uttering the same phrases over and over. His footsteps clip clopping, louder then quieter, louder then quieter as he paced not far from where they were hiding. She heard the distinctive crunch and click of a gun being reloaded, then silence.

Hugo got to his feet and walked to the door. Annie could just make out his small frame in the darkness, she wanted to go to him and pull him back into the safety of her arms, but there was so much stuff in the cupboard she was liable to knock into something and give them both away.

"No es justo," the gunman said.

Hugo cocked his head, his shadowy figure moving so close to the door his ear was pressed against it. Annie bit her tongue. She wanted to shout at him to come back, that it wasn't safe. Her heart was thumping in her chest as though trying to make an escape. Her throat felt thick. She hadn't made it this far to be gunned down in a closet.

The gunman screamed again, forcing Hugo to back up. With his hand on the door, Hugo pushed it open just a fraction of an inch as he flinched. Light streamed in, and there, out in the corridor, dressed all in black, face masked, holding the evillest gun Annie had ever seen, was the gunman. His head turned in the direction of the door. Annie took her cue and grabbed hold of Hugo, dragging him into her arms. If they were going to be shot at, the best Annie could do was make the young boy feel safe.

But he pushed against her, scrambling to be free. His legs kicked out, hitting Annie in the shins with a crunch. Red hot pain like liquid flooded her leg and her arms spasmed, allowing the young boy to break free.

He shot towards the door and pushed it back open, bursting out into the corridor like a bullet himself. Through the open door Annie saw in horror as Hugo pushed at the gunman, hitting out at his legs with tiny, balled fists. The gunman pulled down his mask, his face twisted. He lifted Hugo off the floor with one arm and the young boy hung there like a rag doll.

"Let him go," Annie cried, bursting out of the cupboard, bottle of bleach aimed at the gunman's face.

He looked at Annie with eyes so dark she couldn't see his pupils. There was something about his face that she recognised. Like a c list celebrity sighting or an old school acquaintance. And when Annie tore her eyes away from his face and directed them towards the boy she'd been trying to keep safe, her stomach turned liquid with fear.

Hugo's face was drawn into a huge smile, his lips stretching from ear to ear as he threw his arms around the gunman and gave him a hug.

"No." Annie stumbled back, not able to comprehend what was happening. "No. No. No."

A burst of laughter flew out of Hugo's mouth which almost distracted Annie away from the gun that was being lifted and pointed at her face.

TWENTY

Time stood still. The world echoed around Annie like a stop-motion movie and she was merely looking though the viewfinder of the camera. Hugo's laugh deepened as though slowed to half-speed and stretched out like the smile on his face. The gunman's hand lifted, pointing the barrel of the semi-automatic right at Annie's face. She could smell the sulphur. She could taste the thick smoke in the air.

If it *was* a movie, then Annie was sure it was a horror.

All this time, Annie had been trying to save the youngest, most vulnerable member of their group. And here he was in the arms of the killer, and happy about it.

"Estúpida." The gunman echoed Annie's thoughts.

It was now or never.

Pushing off from the tips of her toes, their clammy

grip tight on the tiles, Annie barrelled right into the gunman. Arms outstretched she impacted with his shoulders and forced him away from her. With the weight of Hugo, the man was unbalanced, and he toppled backwards, clinging to the boy as though he was a life preserver. His gun arm twitched upwards, his hands tensed around the trigger as he lost his footing, sending an arc of bullets into the sky.

Annie didn't feel it enter her shoulder as she ducked underneath the gun and ran as fast as she could in the only direction that was safe. She heard the man cry out; Hugo screamed, a loud clatter exploded through the corridor. Something trickled down Annie's arm, tickling her skin, and she brushed it away, surprised to feel wetness on her fingers. They were sticky and red. The metallic smell almost stopped her in her tracks, but somewhere deep in her gut, an animalistic instinct told her to keep running. She burst through the door to the restaurant and collapsed on the hard floor.

IT COULD HAVE BEEN SECONDS LATER, IT COULD HAVE been hours, Annie opened her eyes to a crowd of people looking over her. Their faces all had a greyness to them, sunken eyes, and greasy hair. But Annie felt a sense of relief staring up at them.

"Are you okay?" It was a young man Annie recognised from the pool. He had a fondness for bright swim shorts and splashing his partner where he lay reading a book. Right now, he looked as colourless as the rest of them, his partner beside him, not much better.

"I'm not sure." Annie sat up, her head thumping as the last few minutes came rushing back to her. "We need to barricade the door."

She tried to get up off the floor but the room span around her, making her retch.

"It's done," an older woman replied, her hand on Annie's arm. "You want me to take a look at that?"

The woman nodded at Annie's shoulder. Annie glanced down at it, wondering for a split second why the stolen hoody had changed colour, but it only took a few seconds to realise it wasn't an illusion, it was her blood. Annie retched again and the woman took that as an affirmative that Annie needed help.

She peeled the hoody gently over Annie's head and shoulders, and as the woman worked to stem the flow of blood in Annie's shoulder, she talked softly and calmly, the bedside manner of a nurse.

"You'll be okay," she told Annie. "I think the bullet went all the way through so there's less of a risk of infection. Hopefully with the sun coming up, help will arrive."

"I've called the police," Annie replied, biting so hard on her bottom lip that it started bleeding too. "They're surrounding the hotel. What happened in here? I heard shots. There were so many of them I didn't think anyone would be left alive."

The woman dabbed a napkin with a splash of vodka and told Annie to prepare herself.

"He gathered us all in here," she said, holding the napkin against Annie's shoulder with surprising force. "He was angry. But he didn't shoot at us. He shot upwards, at the ceiling. At the doors. He kept shouting at us all though. Expecting us to understand. But of course, we're all English and our limited vocabulary is embarrassing."

She gave a wry little laugh and Annie would have agreed if she'd been able to open her mouth without swearing at the pain radiating down her arm.

"He took the staff away," she went on, ripping a section of tablecloth into a thin strip. "Shouting more at them than he did to us. We heard shots and I don't know what happened to the staff. We've been lucky here, really. Told us in broken English to stay here and not move or he'd shoot us. So that's what we've done. Until you arrived."

Sucking air in through her teeth, Annie closed her eyes and pictured the shooter she'd come face to face with. Under the outfit, he'd looked young. No older than Samu or Anders. His face had been wrinkled with anger, but beneath that Annie could picture a man in pain, it was something about the way his eyes had searched Annie's.

"Was it the man in black?" she asked. "Wearing a hat and a bandana mask, I think it was blue and black. Tall. Broad?"

"Yes, that's him," the woman replied. "Local man.

182

Well, Spanish anyway. Maybe not local. I don't know. I'm just guessing. What happened to you?"

Annie told her the short version of her day. From the boat trip to the cafe.

"And the boy seemed okay?" the woman asked.

Annie nodded, her stomach churning. "More than okay. It was as though he'd been waiting for the opportunity."

"I hope he's safe." The woman worked in silence for a moment, the others from the restaurant had dispersed back to where they'd been sitting before Annie unceremoniously burst in. "I'm Mary, by the way."

"Annie. Thanks for your help." Annie looked down at her arm, bandaged and not bleeding anymore, and pulled the warm jumper back over her head, slotting only her good arm in the sleeve.

Her mind ticked over as Mary cleared away the offcuts and bloody napkins. Maybe Hugo had felt safer with someone who spoke his language. Or maybe the realisation that Annie had come to was true. Hugo was never a guest at the hotel, he was part of the problem.

He's four, O'Malley. Swift was there again, popping into her head like a jack-in-the-box.

Annie accepted a glass of water from Mary and a hand up. She ached, she was cold, but she was still alive. The door had been blocked with tables and chairs and one of the benches that Annie had danced at on their first night. Sangria in one hand, her sister in the other. They'd sung and laughed and danced until the early hours. And now it was the early hours again and Annie wished she could go back and relive the first few days of the holiday. She'd be less angry at Mim. No, not at Mim, it wasn't anger at Mim that burned in her belly. It was anger at her mum and dad.

Annie walked to the window, looking down over the cliffs below. The turquoise sea was calm, lapping against the rock face as though it knew no better. Taking her phone from her pocket, Annie saw she had five missed calls from Swift. She swiped the screen and dialled his number.

"O'Malley, are you okay to talk?" Swift answered almost immediately again.

"Yes," she replied, perching on the windowsill, her shoulder throbbing. "I'm in the restaurant so I'm not sure how great the reception will be. What's the news with the police? Are they in the building yet? Mim and Ricky and a couple of others are in the basement."

Annie heard Tink and Page in the background, the ringing of phones and the clatter of keyboards. The office was waking up. It was weird to think that people were still going about their normal lives when the guests at the hotel were stuck in a recurring nightmare. A limbo land of the worst kind.

"Annie, we found something," Swift said with a rustling of paper. "Page has been searching the CCTV of the hotel, it's set up online, thankfully, but I still practically had to offer up my body to the hotel owner to get her to let me download it all."

"And that offer worked, did it?" Annie felt lighter talking to Swift, away from the terror of the gunman outside the door. "Or did she make you pay extra?"

There was a beat of silence before Swift spoke.

"Glad to see you've not lost your sense of humour, O'Malley," he said, stoically. "I'll have you know it's my best bargaining chip at the moment."

"I'll bear that in mind if you need to negotiate with the gunmen," she added, trying hard not to laugh.

The kind of laugh that stemmed from fear and hysteria was not a road Annie wanted to take. She knew it would be a dead end with a steep drop waiting for her, just like the one outside the window.

"Shut up," Swift said, the smile apparent in his voice, until he dropped it and carried on. "Anyway. The CCTV covers the front and back gates of the hotel. We focused on the back gate as that's the one you said was broken. You're right. There are three gunmen in total. One of them arrived not long after ten, slipped through the gate at the back, fired at staff almost immediately. Another two arrived about an hour later. Same gate."

Annie blew out a stream of air. She felt sick.

"But get this," Swift went on. "We rewound the tape back a couple of nights and watched what happened at the gate. Nice hotel, by the way. And bikini."

Annie felt her face flush and turned to look out the window so no one would see.

Not the best time to be flirting, Swift.

"And?" she prompted, ignoring the comment. "The gate?"

"Yeah." Swift cleared his throat. "You were right when you said you thought someone inside had broken the gate. A few nights ago a man was outside, he kept his hood up and his face away from the cameras, but he was talking to someone through the bars of the gate. And that same person, the next night, was out there at the gate pushing something large down by the latch. We couldn't see what they were using but it snapped away and the gate dropped open."

"It was a spade," Annie reminded Swift. "A child's spade."

"Makes sense," Swift went on. "Because the person we saw interfering with the latch was a small boy."

"Hugo?" Annie asked, her temperature dropping rapidly.

"Swift, Hugo is with one of the shooters now," Annie went on. "What did you find out about him?"

"Apart from being Samu's nephew, not much yet. There's limited history on him, understandably, given his age."

"What about Sofia, his mum?" Annie asked.

"When we saw it was a young boy, we assumed it was the family you talked about and with her relation

186

to Samu we did a more thorough search on Sofia's history," he said, and Annie heard him take a stuttered breath.

"What? What is it Swift?"

"Sofia's full name is Sofia Emilie Theobald. Samu is Samuel Thomas Theobald."

The name itched inside Annie's head. *Theobald.* She knew it, she just couldn't place it. *Thomas Theobald.* Then a red hot knife twisted itself in her chest as the pieces starting to fall into place.

"Oh my god," she gasped. "As in Thomas Theobald from our first ever case?"

The Theobald case was notorious in the UK. Children stolen and sold to European traffickers. During Annie's first case they'd found one of Theobald's stolen children and reunited him with his birth parents after over a decade apart. The head honcho, Thomas Theobald, had been jailed fifteen years previously, putting Sofia and Samu at around ten when it happened.

"The very same." Swift sounded grave.

"Swift, I need to find Sofia," she whispered. "I think she's in on it, and I know who she might be targeting. Can you search the recent CCTV, last night and this morning and tell me where she went after she was shot at by the pool?"

"We did," he said. "Tink was way ahead of me. It looks like Sofia was caught in accidental crossfire, she was hit but okay from what we could gather. Two of the gunmen found her and helped her up and indoors."

Annie swallowed bile as it burned her throat. This was a woman she'd spent time with on the boat, had spoken to and laughed with. What if Sofia hadn't come to the hotel to escape the humdrum of everyday life like all the other guests, what if she'd come here to steal children and traffic them across the continent.

"Annie," Swift went on, his voice grave. "If you see her, don't approach her. They gave her a gun. She's armed."

TWENTY-ONE

"I'D TELL YOU, DON'T BE A HERO, O'MALLEY," Swift said. "But you won't listen to me. So what I will say is please be careful. No one is worth risking your life over."

"You are, Joe," she whispered quietly enough that he couldn't hear her, her whole-body tensing.

Annie hung up and slipped her phone away. She looked around the restaurant at the tired guests and their scared faces. And taking them in, Annie realised for the first time since she set foot back in the hotel after the dolphin trip that she hadn't seen a single child. Where was the boy who'd splashed her on her first morning in the pool? Where were the twins who'd played peekaboo with her the first night in the restaurant? The young siblings who'd been on the cusp of adulthood, their hormones wreaking havoc with their emotions as they'd sat still and silent on their phones most of the holiday.

Annie caught Mary's eye and called her over to the window. The sun was almost fully up and the heat permeating through the glass was too much. Annie slipped off the hoody and sat in her bikini top and shorts.

"How are you feeling?" Mary asked her. "I'd like to offer you some paracetamol but it's in my room."

Annie had forgotten all about her shoulder and shrugged it off.

"Where are the kids?" she asked, nodding to the groups of guests.

"The kids?" Mary's eyebrows knotted together, and she moved in closer to Annie. "I'm talking quietly as there are a few parents in here and they've been distraught."

Annie glanced again at the guests, spotting the faces of those frightened by something other than their own mortality. It was easy to see now she knew to look for it. Gaunt cheeks, hollow eyes, the nervousness in their movements. Annie couldn't imagine what they were going through.

"There's a sitting service at the hotel," Mary went on. "Staff members paid to babysit, essentially. There's also a crèche for the younger ones for the evening, so the parents can enjoy the entertainment with a drink."

Panic was seeping into Annie's pores.

"Where is this crèche?"

"Down the corridor from the bedrooms," Mary replied. "The right wing of the hotel."

Annie remembered the way Samu had been upstairs when she'd first caught sight of him. She'd thought he was up there firing at guests, but maybe it was something more sinister.

"Thanks Mary." Annie stood from the window ledge. "There's a small boat down in the cove. It's a good escape route."

Mary shook her head. "I'm needed here. We won't all fit on a small boat, and I've got medical knowledge that has come in handy so far."

"Okay," Annie agreed.

"You said you'd called the police?" Mary asked.

"They're on their way. Just stay put and barricade the door behind me."

"Where are you going? You're hurt. Why don't you stay here with us until help arrives?"

Annie looked at Mary's face, touched by the camaraderie she was displaying.

"I think we've been ushered in here for a reason," she said. "Made to feel so scared that we stay out of the way."

"Why?" Mary asked, her words tumbling out in a flurry. "Why did you ask about the children? Is there something going on with the children?"

Her face looked pinched.

"It might be nothing," Annie replied, shaking her head. "But I can't sit here and not help, just in case. You stay here, then. Make sure everyone is okay. And try to keep people calm."

Mary chewed her lip and sighed. But she rose

with Annie and together they moved the tables and chairs away from the door.

"Be safe." Mary shut the door behind her, and Annie was on her own.

———

THE CORRIDOR WAS EMPTY, ANNIE RAN AS QUIETLY AS she could towards the reception area and the stairs. Flies buzzed around the desk; the smell of blood thick in the air. Annie held her breath and headed across the tiles to the bottom step. Chancing her luck, she took them quickly and rounded the landing of the first floor, heart beating so hard she could feel it in her neck.

A shout rang out. Bullets were fired. Annie didn't take time to think about it, she followed the noise down past the doors to the bedrooms to the end of the walkway. A large, painted clown's face smiled down at her from the door. *Guardería* was written in type-face across the wall above it. Behind the door it sounded as though the children were rousing. A patter of cries and the hushing of someone trying to keep them quiet.

Annie frowned. She turned the handle and pushed the door open just wide enough to peek in. What she saw, chilled her to the bone.

Sofia.

"Please don't hurt them," Annie called, pushing the door open and stepping into the room.

192

Sofia marched over, gun aloft and slammed the door shut behind Annie. Swift had been right in saying Sofia had been caught in the crossfire, but his evaluation of her injuries was way off. Blood soaked all the way through her t-shirt and stained the top of her shorts. Annie felt a surge of compassion for the woman who was now so pale the skin under her tan was blue.

"¿Qué estás haciendo?" Sofia spat at her.

Annie held her hands in the air to show she wasn't a threat as Sofia waved the gun in her face.

"I don't understand, Sofia," Annie said, highlighting her lack of Spanish, but also the dread building in her at the idea of Sofia taking the handful of children in the room.

The younger ones looked up at the women from their beds, wide eyed and silent. They must have sensed the danger, or else they were still too sleepy to scream. Annie didn't know much about kids, only that they were very noisy, so to be in a room full of quiet ones was making her as uneasy as Sofia's gun was.

"You've ruined it," Sofia said in broken English. "Where's Hugo?"

Tears sprang into Sofia's eyes, and she wiped them away angrily with her free hand.

"I don't know," Annie said truthfully.

Maybe if Sofia didn't know he was safely with her partner in all of this, Annie could use him as leverage. She edged forward, towards Sofia, her arms still up in surrender.

"Get back," Sofia hissed. "You can't be here."

Annie paused, dropping her hands slightly.

"I can't let you do this," she said, taking a small step towards Sofia. "You're hurt, Sofia. You need help."

"I need Hugo," Sofia replied. "You need to STOP."

Hugo, Annie realised, was the key to their operation. He'd befriended a lot of these young children, he'd broken the gate to give the gunmen access, he was helping Sofia move them from the hotel to...

"Where are you taking them, Sofia?" Annie asked. "I know your name. Sofia Theobald. I know about your dad and I know Samu is your brother."

Annie was guessing at her relationship with Thomas Theobald but the shock on Sofia's face confirmed what she'd been thinking.

"I... I... you don't know what you're saying." Sofia stuttered her words, her eyes glazing over.

"Sofia, you don't need to do this." Annie moved another step closer. "Think of these poor children. What about Hugo? How would you feel if it was Hugo?"

At the mention of her son, Sofia's face clouded, she looked at Annie again and the daze lifted.

"Don't you talk about my son," she spat, eyes narrow. "Lo dejas fuera."

Sofia lifted the gun higher, clicking off the safety. Annie took a step away from Sofia, feeling the door against her back. Her mind ran away with her. Annie had heard a tirade of shots fired and angry shouts coming from this direction, that's why she'd run towards them. But Sofia didn't have an automatic weapon, she had a handgun, the same as Samu.

"Is there someone else here with you?" Annie asked, looking around the room for hiding places. "Who is it you're working with? Your father had connections, have you taken over from him, is that it? Who else is here?"

Apart from the small beds which were far too low for anyone to crawl under, and a bank of narrow lockers, there was no place for anyone to hide.

"Who did you shoot?" Annie went on, thinking of the staff member who would have been in here looking after the children. "I heard gunshots."

"I didn't," Sofia's face fell. "I not shoot."

Her eyes darted over Annie's shoulder towards the door then she doubled over, clutching her stomach.

"Sofia," Annie ignored the gun and went to the young woman.

"I'm hurt," she gasped. "I'm shot. It was me."

Annie helped her drop to the floor, kicking the gun out of reach as it slipped from Sofia's fingers. She lifted the young woman's jumper and a torrent of blood oozed from a large wound.

"Shit, Sofia, who did this?" Annie looked around for something to stem the flow.

She grabbed a pillow from an empty bed and held it tightly to Sofia's stomach as the children watched on. Annie was so out of her depth, she felt sick. She couldn't calm these kids down, and she could feel the tension climbing the walls of the room as they started to get anxious.

"You're going to be okay," she said, to every single person around her, pushing hard down onto the pillow.

Sofia lay her head down, her eyes fluttering.

"No," Annie yelled. "You stay with me, you hear. Hugo needs you."

Annie wasn't sure if Hugo even belonged to Sofia, or if he was a victim of the trafficking team working their way around the hotel. But at that moment, Annie needed a reason for Sofia to stay alive.

A blast of heady terror radiated through her as the door burst open and Samu and Anders ran in. She looked across the floor, trying to reach the gun she'd kicked out of reach, but it was no good.

The two men marched into the room and were beside Annie and Sofia in less than two steps.

"What have you done?" Anders asked, his eyes large on Annie.

"*Me?*" she cried. "You're the ones with the guns. You're the ones who shot the staff. You're the ones who're here to take *them*."

Annie looked around at the children, who were all starting to cry. They ranged from the small sniffles of a child too scared to make a noise to the high-pitched screams of the babies that Annie couldn't block out.

Samu covered his ears with his hands, screaming at Annie to move.

"Get her up," he shouted to Anders. "Move her, now. Sofia, Hugo is on the boat, they're leaving. We need to go. NOW."

That's why they left the keys in the boat, for a quick getaway.

Sofia's eyes fluttered open again, her mouth trying to move its way around words but not quite working. Anders dropped to his knees beside Annie and slid out of his shirt, tying it tightly around Sofia's waist. He scooped her up, one arm over his shoulder, and hauled himself and Sofia to standing.

Annie took her chance to scuttle across the floor, grabbing the gun and holding it aloft. It felt bulky in her hands, completely alien to her. But she managed to point it at Samu, her finger millimetres away from the trigger.

"I can't let you get away." Her hands were shaking, the gun rattling and giving away her nerves.

They may have been going to leave these children in the safety of the hotel, but Annie knew if they escaped now, they'd very likely disappear and never be caught. They needed to be stopped, they needed to never be able to do this again. They were needed to get to the top of the chain. Theobald had passed his business down the family line, but there was no way Sofia and Samu were the top dogs.

Samu looked from his sister to Annie, his face stained with the blood from the head wound Annie had given him. His eyes were black, boring into Annie with the force of a bullet.

"And I can't let you stop us." He inched the gun he had trained on Annie slightly to the right and pulled the trigger.

TWENTY-TWO

PRIOR TO THAT MORNING THE IDEA OF BEING SHOT AT was reserved for books and television. Now Annie lay on the floor of a creche, crying children surrounding her, brain working overtime to try and feel the newest bullet hole.

Her right shoulder ached where she'd landed on bullet hole number one. Diving to the floor as Samu had fired at her, Annie had thumped heavily on the tiles. Her own gun had skittered across the floor, slipped out of her fingers with the sweat. She moved tentatively, her head thundering with dehydration and tiredness.

It's known that baby's cries are pitched so the human ear cannot ignore them. Annie felt like they were inside her head and the idea of poking her fingers so far into her ears they popped her eardrums was a good one. If only she could lift her arms.

They're at the boat.

Annie fought the pain to remember what Samu had said. They were leaving on the boat. They were getting away. She let out an almighty roar, and pushed up from the tiles, collapsing onto her knees. Blood pulsed out of her original shoulder wound, oozing thickly past the makeshift bandage and down her arm. And her left hand was like a deadweight on the end of her wrist. Gritting her teeth, Annie looked down, bile rising as she saw the mess the bullet had left. Her forearm looked like a kebab skewer, pink and raw. Through the impact point, Annie could see her own sinew and tendons, the bone shattered where the bullet had ripped through the skin. She swallowed down the sickness and rested her head on her bent knees while the stars faded from her eyes. It could have been worse, at least he'd missed the arteries. Though it was bleeding, it wasn't pumping the blood out with life ending force.

"Es seguro?" The voice made Annie jump.

She peeled her eyes open, trying to see past the jackhammer in her head making her eyes dizzy, to a young woman with staff uniform sneaking out from inside one of the narrow lockers. One by one, the other lockers opened revealing scared looking children a little older than the babes who were crying.

"I'm sorry, I don't speak Spanish." Annie rubbed the knuckles of her working hand into her eyes, struggling to her feet. "Are you okay?"

"Me?" The young woman looked at Annie,

answering her in perfect English. "I'm more worried about you. You've been hit."

Annie tried not to look at her broken arm. She couldn't see anything to wrap it up with except a pink blanket with the motif of a bunny wrapped tightly in a small girl's hands, and Annie wasn't about to steal from a child.

"I'm fine." She pressed a hand over the wound instead, doubling over with the pain. "At least, I will be. What happened?"

"There was a man." The woman was talking to Annie as she tended to the youngest of the crying children. "He came here, he had a child with him. And a gun. When I first heard the shooting, I tried my best to keep the children quiet. We've been hiding out in here since last night. It's hard though, you know. I think the gunman must have heard the little ones and I heard him coming and hid as many of the children as I could. It wasn't enough though. I should have taken them all.

"I watched through the door as he tried to grab the ones who were old enough to walk. But then the woman arrived and they started arguing. She tried to take the young boy, I think it was his mum, I've seen them here on holiday, but the man shot her, right here."

She gestured to her stomach.

"You did an amazing job keeping these kids safe," Annie said, looking at the three older children who'd hidden away in the lockers.

They would never forget this night, none of the children here would. But at least they were safe, for now. They could go back to their parents and grandparents and be wrapped in the arms of those who loved them and cared for them. The same couldn't be said for those children who were taken by Theobald and his gangs. Smuggled between countries to rich men to do with as they pleased. Organ donors. Sex traffickers. Modern day slavery. Annie found it hard to comprehend what some human beings are capable of doing to others. The entitlement of those with money was deranged.

"Help is on the way," Annie went on. "Stay safe."

Before she could listen to another person telling her to stay with them, Annie limped out of the crèche and pulled the door closed behind her.

Something wasn't adding up. The different guns. Sofia being shot. Samu and Anders in all of this. Annie's brain was trying to keep up, but blood loss wasn't helping. She let her mind run away as she limped down the stairs to the reception and past the desk to the poolside.

Annie needed to let Swift know they were planning to escape by sea. She tried to get her phone out her pocket but it was on her left hip. Her left hand was useless, her right hand didn't reach over that far with the bullet wound in her shoulder.

"Argh," Annie screamed in frustration as she shuffled towards the gate and the stairs to the dock.

She wanted to sit down, tiredness enveloping her

like a warm blanket and a cup of cocoa. But she couldn't. If she waited here, they'd get away. Be long gone before the police came to help. Where were the police? Why was it taking them so long to infiltrate the hotel? She doubled her pace, slipping on the steps, her good arm reaching out to stop herself from falling.

Samu, Anders, and Sofia stood on the dock below. The two men holding Sofia between them as she slumped forward in their arms. The third gunman was on the boat, Hugo cowering behind his legs. They were shouting in Spanish. Annie didn't know what they were saying but the anger was palpable.

Annie descended slowly, not wanting to draw attention to herself. As she got closer, she could see the guns. Samu and the third gunman were in a deadlock. Samu's handgun pointing at the other man's head. The automatic weapon pointed right back.

What is going on?

Annie lifted her good hand to shield the glare from the sun, scanning the dock and the boat. The three on the dock were facing away, the man on the boat could see her if he looked up. Crouching down behind the scrub, away from the gaze of the third gunman, Annie slowly made her way to the wooden dock. The argument swelled, harsh voices over the gentle rush of the water.

The man on the boat, gun still trained on Samu, started to edge towards the controls. Sofia cried out. Hugo looked between his mum and the man who held him now in a tight grip.

"Papá?" He had started crying now too.

Papa? This man was Hugo's dad? This man had shot at Hugo's mum, was escaping on a boat away from Sofia and her family. What if Annie had it all wrong? What if the gunman wasn't out to kill as many people as he could? What if he had nothing to do with the Theobalds or their smuggling ring? What if he was here to rescue a child that had been taken *from* him?

The different types of guns. The fact they arrived at the hotel separately. The animosity between them all, standing on the dock and the boat. They weren't working together. The gunman was here on his own, and he had what he came for.

It was all happening so fast. Hugo's dad pulled at his arm, dragging him along behind him to the wheel of the boat. Samu ducked out from under Sofia, leaving Anders to hold her up. She stumbled a little, one leg buckling out from under her. Despite Sofia's motives, Annie couldn't stand and watch the young mother fall, so she bolted out from behind the scrub and took Samu's place under Sofia's arm. Her skin was clammy and cold, her cheeks translucent.

"It's okay," Annie said, watching in horror as Samu jumped onto the boat as it started away from the dock.

"Te voy a matar jodidamente," Samu shouted, landing on the boat with a thud and scrambling to his feet.

Samu darted towards the gunman, a scream emitting from his body like none Annie had ever heard before. The man turned, confused by the speed at which Samu was racing towards him. And then the world seemed to slow down.

The gunman lifted the automatic weapon towards Samu, his back against the wheel of the boat, spinning it around in a circle, bringing the boat back towards the dock. Hugo saw his dad about to shoot and ducked out from his grip, running in front of the gun. Sofia cried out, summoning up the strength of a bear to lift herself from Anders and Annie and stumble onto the boat as it scraped the wooden jetty.

Shots fired into the blazing morning sun and the jetty punctured the hull with an ear splitting screech. Hugo tripped, unbalanced by the boat as it jettisoned away from the dock, falling into the sea. Annie didn't even think about what she was doing. She ran to the edge of the jetty and dived into the water. Hugo was sinking fast, dragged down by his clothes. He may have been a good swimmer, but shock and tiredness and the speed at which he'd ended up in the water made the little boy no match for the power of the sea. Annie kicked with her legs, using her good arm to reach as far forward as she could. Her fingers brushed Hugo's t-shirt and they clenched, grabbing as much of the fabric as she was able to.

Her lungs ached, her shot shoulder stung, her broken arm felt like it was disintegrating into the Mediterranean Sea, but Annie tugged at Hugo's t-shirt and stopped him from his downward descent. She righted her body, kicking out with her legs to get to the surface. It wasn't far. She could see the sun glaring off the tips of the waves. One more kick. Annie felt her chest concave. Just one more kick. She burst through the water, gasping for air, filling her lungs until they hurt. Using the last of her strength, Annie lifted Hugo out of the water and pushed him up onto the dock and into Anders' waiting arms. She caught sight of Sofia, slumped on the boat, blood pooling underneath her.

As she lifted the boy to safety, without the use of both of her arms, Annie felt herself propelled downwards. Trying to kick, she realised she had no strength left. Nothing in the tanks. Two gunshot wounds. Being awake for over twenty-four hours. Shock. Adrenaline fading. Annie sank deeper. Pictures flashed in her mind. Her parents together, happy. Mim, last night, talking of their undercover work. Sunday the cat weeing in her pot plant. And Swift. Of course, Swift. Joe's crooked smile as he looked up at her through his unruly eyebrows. His strong arms as he hugged her. The blue of his eyes that she'd never again compare to the colour of the Med. Annie's lungs couldn't hold out any longer. She'd sank before she'd filled them. She'd taken one last breath and it wasn't enough.

She closed her eyes and prepared for the darkness.

TWENTY-THREE

SWIFT BARGED HIS WAY PAST A GROUP OF ONLOOKERS who'd crowded around the entrance to the hotel, their necks craning to see inside. The white walls lit up with the flashing blue lights from the emergency vehicles, casting the building into a giant soft mint. Though the police tape held the crowd back from the scenes inside, the onlookers were as difficult to penetrate as the vines around sleeping beauty's castle.

"Move," Swift shouted, elbowing them to get through. "Out of my way. I'm UK police."

"Swift?" A woman's voice cut through the noise of the crowds. "Is that you?"

He turned to look where it had come from and saw a young woman covered in dried blood.

"Yes," he said, pushing past people to get to her. "Who are you? Where's Annie?"

The woman bit her bottom lip and tears filled her eyes.

"Charlie. They won't let me back in," she said. "I need to find Ricky. I need to make sure he's okay."

Swift put his hands on the girl's shoulders. She wasn't going to know where Annie was, she had been sent to safety before Annie went back to the hotel. "Go and get yourself checked out. I'm heading in now; I'll get them to update you as soon as I know anything."

He didn't have time to stay with her and make sure she was okay. Swift had one thing on his mind and pinpoint focus as he ducked under the tape right into a police officer with a clipboard.

"You can't go in there," the uniformed man said in perfect English, spotting Swift as a foreigner with his sweaty face and lack of tan. "Behind the line, please."

Swift fumbled in his pocket and drew out his badge.

"Police," he said with more gusto than he felt.

The officer took it, studying it for longer than he needed.

"You the one who called it in from England?" he asked, eyebrows drawn at the information on Swift's ID.

"Yeah, that's me," Swift replied, grabbing his badge back as it was offered. "Can I get through?"

"You got here quickly." The officer was studying Swift now he'd given back the ID.

"What can I say?" Swift shrugged. "I'm a conscientious worker. Can I, just…?"

He indicated the open door where paramedics and police milled around just inside.

"It's out of your jurisdiction." The officer was having none of it.

Swift did a double take, not quite comprehending the no.

"But I've got people in there I know. Work colleagues," he said, hands out, pleading. "Please. You have to let me in."

"So are you here with work, or to find the people you know?" The officer shifted his weight. "Because it's a long way to come just to make sure the people you work with are okay."

"I'd have flown to Australia for Annie if it meant I could make sure she was okay." Swift felt his face redden and hoped the officer would put it down to the heat.

"Annie?" The officer wasn't paying attention to Swift's blushes. He checked the clipboard in his hands. "Surname?"

The blood rushed from Swift's face pretty quickly. Officers with clipboards at the scene of a crime were there for three reasons: keeping people out, protecting those beyond, taking names of those who were dead or missing.

"O'Malley?" Swift's voice shook.

The officer gave a single nod. "Round to the side entrance," he said, pointing further down the building where another officer stood guarding a sealed door. "There's a family waiting area."

The look that passed between the two police officers was one Swift never wanted to be part of again.
He'd given that look to family members before. The
I'm so sorry for your loss look. The look that stripped
away the *before* from the *after*.

Swift felt sick. Air escaped his lungs, his knees
felt like they were made of jelly.

"Despejar el camino." The voice sounded like it
was echoing in his ears as the rattle of a gurney came
up behind him. "Clear, please."

The officer put a strong hand on Swift's shoulder
and guided him over and out the way of the main
entrance. Swift didn't want to look, he knew the
sounds of the trolleys, knew why police rather than
paramedics would be wheeling them away from the
scene of a crime. But it was like a scab he couldn't
leave alone. He turned and looked.

A masked policeman pushed a trolley out of the
hotel doors. Sheets covered the body and face of the
person being wheeled to the black ambulance. Swift
couldn't see anything other than the outline of the
body under the sheets, but it was smaller, a female
shape maybe.

"¿Quedan muchos muertos más por venir??" the
paramedic at the private ambulance asked the police
officer.

"Si, un par." The officer handed over the gurney
and pulled down his mask. His face was clammy;
putty coloured and sweaty.

Swift spoke French and Spanish, a testament to

his private school upbringing and parents who wanted him to have a career in international diplomacy. But right at that moment he wanted nothing more than to be oblivious to the deaths that had occurred last night.

More bodies still to come.

More fatalities.

That was many different ways in which he may never see O'Malley again.

"Let me go," Swift barked at the officer who'd stopped him.

Swift moved, shaking the officer's hand away from his shoulder and marching towards the side entrance to the hotel. He was so nervous; his whole body was trembling so much that his teeth clattered in his head.

"This way, please." The officer at the door to the family room spoke with a calm voice that made Swift even more nervous. He wanted normality, not this pussy footing around reserved for difficult conversations.

They walked through the door into a small room used as an office. Swift's skin prickled in bumps at the sharpness of the aircon, and underneath it he could smell the distinct tang of blood. The officer took out a notepad and asked for Swift's name and the name of the family member he was looking for.

He couldn't bear it.

"You've got it wrong," he said to the officer, straightening his shoulders. "I'm here as police."

He took out his badge again, hoping it would

work better this time, and the officer took it with a furrowed brow.

"I recognise your name. You called this in?" the officer said. "I thought you were in the UK?"

Swift nodded, swallowing the thick lump in his throat that was blocking his words.

"Thank you. But you didn't need to come here, we are capable."

"I know," Swift blurted out, not wanting to blow his chances of getting beyond this little room. "I'm here for a friend, the one who called me. She's staying here. She was trying to help. I need to find her."

"Wait here," the officer handed back Swift's badge and left the room through a different door.

Swift had never been one for following rules. He counted to ten and quietly turned the handle.

On this side of the family room lay a whole different world. Gone was the quiet, subdued feeling and the officers with thoughts and prayers. Out in the main reception of the hotel was like an ant run. People buzzed around, mostly covered head to toe in forensic overalls recognisably similar to the ones Evans used back in Norfolk. Uniformed officers, radios buzzing, took statements from guests who looked cold and tired. An older couple sat on plastic chairs; the woman clutched a fluffy looking cat. A couple of paramedics hooked a man on a gurney up to a drip. The man's face looked familiar. Ricky. Swift recognised him from the intel Tink and Page had gathered. Ricky was alive, but barely.

Ducking behind the stairs, Swift held his breath and listened in to a conversation happening over a pool of blood at the desk.

"Personal o invitados?" An officer asked.

Swift's chest tightened. *Staff or guest?*

A forensic worker stopped what they were doing and stood to the officer.

"Este era un miembro del personal, otro miembro del personal en la piscina. Invitados junto al muelle. Hay oficiales allí ahora." They wiped a gloved wrist over their forehead, pushing thick dark, hair from their eyes.

Two staff and one guest so far.

Swift went into work mode, the forensic worker had said there was a casualty down at the dock. Swift needed to find the dock.

"¿Dónde está el muelle de barcos??" He stepped forward, flashing his badge, eyes on the lookout for the officer who'd left him in the family room.

The two men barely looked at Swift, the forensic worker pointed in the direction of the pool. "Pasar la piscina, salir por la puerta, bajar los escalones."

Swift shouted a thanks and ran out of the reception into the boiling sun. It blinded him, glaring across the white coated building and shimmering from the pool. Barely registering the red tint to the water, Swift ran across the tiles to the gate at the bottom, hand up to shield his eyes.

The sounds of beeping radios and Spanish voices filtered up through the brush to the steps. Swift took them as quickly as he could without breaking his neck, craning to see over the dead-looking plants to the dock. Paramedics mixed with police around a battered looking motorboat. A trolley ready to be filled.

Swift scanned the wooden jetty, heart pounding with fear. He could see a group of people huddled together, paramedics kneeling to help them, but couldn't differentiate between the individuals to find the one he so desperately wanted to see.

As Swift rounded the bottom of the steps to the dock a body was being lifted from the sea and placed on the trolley, a sheet pulled over their face.

Annie.

Swift let out a cry and ran forward, stumbling onto the wooden jetty. An officer was blocking his way within seconds.

"You can't be here."

"Annie?" The word tumbled from Swift's lips as he watched the trolley being lifted and carried away.

"Swift?"

Swift turned at the sound of his name.

"Mim," Swift cried, pushing past the officer and racing to Annie's sister. "What's happened? Where's Annie."

Mim extracted herself from the paramedics, her shoulders burnt and peeling. She threw her arms around him, sobbing into his shoulder.

"Oh, Swift." She couldn't stop crying. "I'm so glad you're here."

"Where's Annie?" he asked again. He wanted to be able to comfort Mim, she quite clearly needed it, but his mind was buzzing like it was full of flies, unable to focus on anything except Annie.

"I tried to pull her from the water," Mim cried. "I had a hold of her hair. I knew there was something wrong. I felt it in here and I ran as fast as I could. But there was so much going on. The boat. The blood. The people in the water."

She pumped her fist against her chest.

"Mim?" Swift was pleading with her now. "Please, where is Annie?"

"I'm here, Swift."

Annie appeared on the deck of the boat, shivering cold and wrapped in a damp towel. Her hair hung damp around her shoulders, her face puffy and burnt.

"Annie?" Swift and Mim turned together, calling her name.

"Still standing," she laughed, the sweet sound turning to a hacking cough.

A paramedic appeared behind her, tutting, ushering her to the benches at the back of the boat to sit down. Swift leapt over the side of the boat and gathered Annie up in his arms away from the medical officer. Not caring that anyone was watching, not caring that he may be in for a heck of a lot of trouble when he got back to the UK, and not caring that Annie smelt like a football sock that had been left in a hot car, Swift pressed his lips to her forehead and held her as tightly as he dared.

Annie was safe. She was alive. She was in his arms.

And for a moment, Swift felt safe too.

"Until someone can tell me what is going on here. You're all under arrest." The harsh voice made both Annie and Swift jolt.

She peeled out from under his arms, and they turned to look at the officer in question. It was the man who'd left Swift in the family room, red faced and panting.

"We have three people dead and a whole lot of questions." He caught sight of Swift over the side of the boat. "And you should know better. So until further notice, nobody leaves, nobody even moves."

Over on the dock, Swift watched as a young woman hugged a boy tightly, tears streaming down her face as paramedics tried to work on her stomach. Swift recognised the woman as Sofia and the boy must be Hugo.

But who was the man clinging to the boy's other hand? And why did he look so familiar to Swift?

TWENTY-FOUR

ANNIE COULD STILL FEEL THE HEAT OF SWIFT'S LIPS on her forehead. The fleeting moment when all she could feel was the comfort of his arms. In all the confusion, her lungs aching with water, her mind foggy with pain, Annie wasn't entirely sure she hadn't just dreamt it all.

The last thing she remembered clearly was sinking to the depths of the Mediterranean Sea, trying to think happy thoughts as her air ran out. She had felt a hand gripping her hair and pulling painfully, but after that it was darkness until the sound of Swift calling her name had brought her round.

"Sit." The police officer motioned to Annie and Swift and Mim to take a seat on the wooden jetty with Anders, Sofia, and Hugo's dad.

All of them had been patted down for weapons and all except Annie and Mim and Swift had been shackled with hand and leg cuffs. Hugo had been ushered away by the paramedics, determined to get to treat at least one of their patients who was still breathing. Sofia hadn't had the energy to put up much of a fight, but Annie could see the pain in the young woman's eyes.

"Sofia?" Annie went to sit next to her, taking Sofia's hand in her own.

"I'm sorry, Annie." Sofia looked at her feet, not able to meet Annie's eyes.

Swift sat down on Annie's free side, leaving a gap between them. Annie felt the coolness of the distance and looked over at her boss.

"Thank you," she said, her voice croaking. "For being here."

Swift shuffled closer, his eyes searching Annie's face. "I had no choice."

She knew he meant it, whatever his reasons for coming, they weren't work related. He had to come to Spain because of her.

"We have three people dead," the police officer began, walking back and forth in front of them. "Two staff and one guest. We have a hotel full of petrified holidaymakers who will never return to our beautiful country. Someone here needs to talk, and they need to do it quickly."

The officer spoke with a lilt of a Spanish accent, but his English was perfect. Annie looked across the line of survivors, as in the dark as the police were, but registering the missing person with a heavy heart.

"Where's Samu?" she asked, quietly.

Sofia's handcuffs clinked as she dropped her face into her hands.

"He didn't make it," she cried through her fingers.

Annie felt her stomach turn to liquid. *He didn't make it.* Had she caused his death in any way, hitting him over the head? What was his part in all of this?

"He jumped in after Hugo too," Sofia replied, sniffing. "But he'd been shot. Luis shot him."

She spat the words out towards Hugo's dad. Luis looked up, shrugging one shoulder as though he'd squashed a beetle and not shot a man.

"May I speak?" Swift raised his hand like he was a schoolboy in a lesson.

"No," the officer cut Swift down with a single word. "Sofia, you talk. What were you doing here, I'm sure it wasn't a holiday?"

Swift huffed and leant back, the warmth of his arm stinging Annie's sunburn. She dropped the damp towel from around her shoulders, lifting her hands to cover her bare skin instead. Still in just her bikini top and shorts, she felt a bit exposed, but the towel had been making her cold. Before she could argue, Swift unbuttoned his short-sleeved shirt and slipped it around her shoulders, leaving his own bare torso open to the sun's burning rays.

"Thank you," Annie whispered, pulling the shirt around her chest.

"We came here to hide from Luis," Sofia said, gently. "My family, they're not good people. They forced me to marry Luis when I was sixteen. His family are rich and at first it was okay. He'd buy me things, treat me well. But our families wanted us to work together, and I thought I was done with that when... when I was younger, but all this time my grandparents had just been waiting to marry me off so I could help them out with the family business. I'm not proud of what I've done, but it's all I've ever known. Then, when I fell pregnant, I knew I couldn't do what I was doing anymore, so after Hugo was born we ran. Luis has been chasing me ever since.

"I thought we'd be safe here for a little while. Hugo deserves some fun, he's such a wonderful little boy. But then Samu turned up a couple of days ago, pretending to know something about dolphins. Anders here runs the company; they know each other from school. But Samu warned me that Luis knew where I was and was coming to get me. He pleaded with me to leave, brought a bag of stuff for me and Hugo. Even set up a pretend dolphin watching trip to get us away. Hugo had to pretend he didn't know them. It's been so hard on him that I wanted him to have a holiday. A proper holiday. He was loving being a little boy."

Her breathing stuttered and she took a moment to regain her composure. The duffle bag wasn't full of guns, it was full of clothes. Annie felt sick.

"If we'd gone with him, none of this would have happened. Nobody would be dead. I'm so sorry. I'm a bad person just like my dad was, just like my whole family are. I wanted to get away from them, but you can't run away from who you really are."

Luis scoffed.

"You're no better than me," Sofia screamed at him, making Annie jump. Swift slipped his hand in Annie's and gave it a squeeze. "You don't love me. You never loved me. And you certainly don't love your son. You're just prepping him to work for you. That's all. You want him to do your dirty work and I've had enough. Hugo showed me what love really is, and you are NOT IT."

"Sofia," Swift said, ignoring the apoplectic face of the police officer. "You're not inherently evil. You can't be. You're not related to Thomas Theobald or any of his family. They trafficked children, Sofia. Their business is in children. You were one of those stolen from their parents, forced to work in awful circumstances."

"But I'm Sofia Theobald," she stuttered.

"Thomas took you away from your family when you were just a child." Swift stood up, circling around to face Sofia and dropping to her eye level. "Both you and Samu were taken within days of each other, too young to remember anything different. Both of you destined for somewhere in Europe, some family in need of organs or gangs in need of…"

He didn't finish his sentence; he didn't need to.

"But for some reason or other, Thomas kept you both," Swift went on. "Perhaps he knew he could marry you off, though I'm not sure why he felt he needed to prep such a young girl for that, not when you were already working for him. And Samu was a pawn used to trap future boys with offers of friendship and fun. You were both victims, Sofia. You've got a family back in the UK who've never stopped looking for you."

Sofia's mouth dropped open, but no words came out. She was pale, clammy, shaking. Annie was shocked too, but it wasn't her in the middle of this.

"Don't think this makes a difference," Luis gestured, his chin tilted towards Sofia. "You're mine no matter who your parents are. Thomas promised you to me, and you will never get away from me. You or Hugo."

"You killed three people, Luis." Sofia was sobbing. "You're going to jail."

Luis scoffed again, tilting his head in the direction of the officer who was watching the whole charade play out.

"You *know* my family," he said. "You won't be arresting me if you know what's good for you. There's no proof I shot anyone."

"Who are you?" Swift asked, standing tall, hands on his hips, the bare chest and six pack not giving him much authority around those who were clothed. "Why did Thomas Theobald keep hold of Sofia just to marry her to you?"

"My family are an old Majorcan family." Luis spoke with such calmness it sent a chill though Annie's bones. "One of the oldest on the island. We're in imports and exports mainly, but my father knows a lot of important people."

Annie could tell what he was saying, without Luis implicitly saying it. He was mafia. A family of generations of child traffickers. Theobald wanted to join forces with Luis' family to build his business and Sofia was his payment.

"Please, sir." Sofia was beside herself. "Arrest him. He's killed three people."

"I'll need you all to come down to the station to give statements," the officers said, looking pointedly at Swift. "That includes you."

He took Luis by the arm and led him away first, but as Annie watched them leave, she saw them laughing together. The kind of laughter that betrayed law and order.

"You'll be okay, Sofia," Annie said, as the young mother was led away too. "We'll make sure you're reunited with Hugo. And we can take you to your family. Your real family."

Sofia chewed her cheek, her face gaunt.

"I don't deserve a good family," she said, letting herself be taken.

Annie looked to Swift, her brow creased. "I can't believe Sofia was taken and abused. She truly believed she was a Theobald. Imagine thinking you're related to a family like that."

Swift, his hand still holding Annie's, waited until Anders had been led away by the remaining officer and turned to Annie and her sister.

"Sofia has done some awful things in her life." He rubbed his free hand over his face. "She has been a part of their organisation for years. So I think you should brace yourself that the Spanish authorities may not go easy on her because she did a lot of her work in this country. I knew I recognised Luis when I saw him. His mugshot is all over the Interpol sites. He's wanted in a lot of different countries but here he can do what he likes. Sofia will be made to pay the price for wanting out."

"But…" Annie started, but Swift held up a hand in surrender.

"I know," he said, softly. "I know, it's unfair. Sofia is a victim. I will do what I can to get her home to England where she can be given a fair trial, but you also have to be aware that Luis' family will fight tooth and nail to get her sent away. The information she holds is too powerful. People before her have died for knowing less about the two families."

"What about Hugo?" Annie asked, leading the way up the steps where another officer was waiting for them, Mim right behind her. "He's got nobody to go to. Nobody safe, anyway."

Swift took a moment, turning to look out over the sea. Annie could see the pinkness developing in the skin on his back from the hot sun, a testament to his kindness for giving her his shirt.

"I will do everything I can to make sure Sofia and Hugo are kept together," he said, eventually, turning back to Annie and Mim. "But I'm not the police's favourite at the moment and I'm not best known for my nurturing skills."

"Talking of which," Mim said as they reached the top of the steps and followed the officer to a waiting car. "Who's looking after Sunday while you're out here?"

"Sunday," Annie yelped, climbing in the back of the air-conditioned police car. "You didn't leave him on his own, did you?"

"No," Swift said a little too quickly. "Of course I didn't. That would be foolish."

The heat crept up on Swift's face and Annie was pretty sure the blush wasn't a result of the sunshine.

TWENTY-FIVE

Two months later.
The Devon coast.

SOFIA WIPED THE CHOCOLATE FROM AROUND HUGO'S mouth as he wriggled to break free. With a shout of joy and a cute little giggle, he broke away from his mum's grip, face only half clean, and ran off down the length of the long lawn, Cielo following close on his heels. Sofia laughed and walked back to join Annie, Mim, and Joe as they lounged on deck chairs by the edge of the pool.

The house was grand. Georgian. An estate really, run by a family held together by love and grief, it showed its hand in faded grandeur. Sofia's birth parents had aged tenfold in the sixteen years since she'd been cruelly taken from them. But the joy on their faces when they were reunited was enough to strip back at least a few of those added years. Sofia and Hugo had moved back home with them once they were released from the case and the whole family were moving forward one step at a time.

For Samu's parents, the pain of Swift's news had been a mixed blessing. Given the chance to properly grieve, they'd buried their son in a churchyard with his grandparents. Annie hadn't been able to stay strong for Samu's family. She held onto the guilt of coming out of the whole situation alive. The guilt of believing he'd been a bad man, when all he'd been doing was trying to help his sister. Annie felt that guilt eating away at her like a cancer. She'd eaten very little since the flight home, balancing out the lack of food with generous helpings of whisky.

There had been little time to reconvene with Mim and go over the bombs that she'd dropped about their parents and they weren't about to do it at this reunion. Annie hadn't even spoken to Swift about their under-cover police story. She felt embarrassed that so much had flown past her without her even realising. It was her life and she'd been oblivious. Annie felt stupid. She felt naive. She felt as though everyone was laughing at her behind her back.

But, right now, down here on the Devon coast in a garden that was once again blooming with life and love, Annie felt at peace.

"He's wonderful," she said, sipping a cool glass of Pimms.

"Thank you." Sofia smiled, plonking herself down between Annie and Mim with a weary thump. "He's a little terror, but he's my little terror."

They sat in silence for a few minutes, the birds singing and swooping around them, the wind blowing gently through the summer sun. Annie closed her eyes, relishing the stillness and the calm. Swift had driven them all down that morning and they were due to stay in a cheap B&B overnight, separate rooms on different floors. Annie thought he'd done that deliberately, though he swore it was the only three rooms they'd had left. He'd said it was a good excuse for a getaway when Sofia had called asking to meet with them all.

"I have news from Spain." Sofia didn't look at either Annie or Swift as she broke the silence.

"What?" Swift asked, shifting as upright as he could on a deckchair. "Is it about Luis? I often call for an update, but they're loathe to pass any information on to me. I think I put their noses out of joint because Annie called me and not them at the start of it all."

"Do you even wonder why it took them so long to get to us? Why they were so angry with you for turning up?" Sofia said, the corner of her mouth twisting.

"They were in on it?" Swift whistled through his teeth.

"What have you heard?" Annie asked, trying not to think about the implications of what Sofia was hinting at and watching Hugo dance and cartwheel about the lawn, his little cat batting his swinging ankles.

"Luis is free."

"What?" Swift and Annie said in unison.

"The charges were dropped when the CCTV went missing and the bullets from the scene couldn't be found," Sofia went on. "He didn't spend one night behind bars as far as I could tell. And now he's back out there, free as a bird. It scares me."

"Does he know where your family were from?" Swift asked.

Sofia shook her head. "I was taken from Norfolk. My family moved here a year later. He'd not need to dig hard to find me though. We've got alarms and security measures, but it's Hugo I worry about the most. What I did makes me feel ill, I tricked children into being my friend to make it easier for Thomas to take them. What if Luis comes for Hugo and makes him do the same?"

"You were a child, Sofia," Annie said, softly. "You did what you thought was a good thing. Making friends with kids is kind."

"Not when they're being trafficked." Sofia puffed out her cheeks and picked at the red skin around her thumbnail. "I am talking to a psychotherapist about it though. She's great. It'll take time, but I know I have to work though it for Hugo's sake. He's not going to remember this when he's older and I need to not bring him down."

"Well you're doing a wonderful job so far." Swift was watching Hugo fly around like an airplane.

"There are being no charges filed against any of the Theobald's either," Sofia added. "There's no evidence. They're too clever. It makes my stomach churn to think my grandparents are still out there working the way they do. My dad pulling all the strings in jail because he's got the staff in his pocket. Luis' family are so rich, they own half the police force out there, and they pay off the ones they need to over here."

Annie felt a chill. As long as the Theobald's were working, Sofia and Hugo weren't safe. She had a huge amount of evidence on the organised crime gang, and they wouldn't think twice about putting a bullet between her eyes to keep it secret. Annie didn't say any of this, but she glanced a look at Swift's tense face and knew he was thinking the same.

"But," Sofia went on, her cheeks pinkening. "Anders is moving over here next month. He's staying here with us until he finds a place of his own and a new job."

"That's great news," Annie said, feeling her own smile at how happy Sofia looked. "He must miss Samu if they'd been friends for so long. It's good for him to be around friends."

"Yep." Sofia smiled. "Friends. Like you guys right? Good friends?"

Swift cleared his throat and shuffled again in his chair. Neither of them had mentioned the moment between them on the boat. The kiss he'd given her, the way he'd held her so tightly she'd been unable to breathe. Not yet anyway.

"The best." Annie filled the awkward silence, smiling at Swift to let him know it was okay to not know what was going on between them.

"You know," Sofia said, looking intently at Annie and Mim. "When I was younger. Before Dad got sent to jail, there was a woman who worked for him that looked just like you two."

Annie drew her brows together. "What do you mean?"

"Same eyes," she said. "Same colour hair. She had your face, Annie, and your physique, Mim. She would come by the house sometimes; she was really kind to me. I never saw her after Dad was sent away. Seeing you both on holiday made me think of her. That's why I struck up a conversation with you on that day, Mim."

Annie felt a chill creep over her body. Could Sofia be talking about their mum? Could her mum have been one of the officers who'd helped jail Thomas Theobald? Surely that would be too coincidental.

Annie looked at Sofia who was wide eyed with the memory. She looked at Mim, then at Swift, who gave her the curious face twist normally reserved for across the bank of desks at work when she'd said something profound.

"I'm glad she was kind to you," Annie replied,

eventually, deciding against bringing it all up now. "Maybe she was one of the good guys."

And maybe she *had* been one of the good guys. Even if it hadn't been Annie's mum working under-cover, and even in the darkest of moments and the cruellest of situations, there are always people who shine like the sun.

Annie glanced again at Swift as he shielded his eyes to watch Charlie, Ricky, Faith, and Ellis walk towards them across the long lawns. She knew he was her ray of light in the bleakest of moments. He had always been there for her since they first met just a few years ago. And, as he felt her watching him and turned his attention back to Annie, Swift smiled in a way that told her she was his ray of light too.

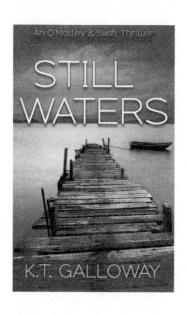

Annie O'Malley & DI Swift return in STILL
WATERS

Still waters run deep

In the midst of a local harvest festival a teen boy
emerges from the legendary Lowanford Lake.
Missing for nearly a week, his skin bloated and
covered in sores from the water, it's a miracle he's
alive.

The legend weaves stories of the lake's miraculous
waters—warm and luminescent—possessing the
power to heal all afflictions.

But the legend is soon questioned when the next day a
body floats to the surface.

And when another teen boy goes missing, Annie and Swift are up against the clock to find him before he succumbs to the water too.

What is it that's luring these young men to the lake? And why are they willing to risk their lives to find it?

THE EIGHTH INSTALMENT IN THE BESTSELLING O'MALLEY AND SWIFT CRIME THRILLER SERIES!

THANK YOU!

Thank you so much for reading One Last Breath. It's hard for me to put into words how much I appreciate my readers. If you enjoyed One Last Breath, I would greatly appreciate it if you took the time to review on your favourite platform.

You can also find me at www.KTGallowaybooks.com

ALSO BY K.T. GALLOWAY

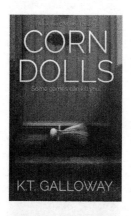

An Annie O'Malley Thriller

WE ALL FALL DOWN

Ring a ring o' roses

K.T. GALLOWAY

An O'Malley & Swift Thriller

THE HOUSE OF SECRETS

K.T. GALLOWAY

An O'Malley & Swift Thriller

THE UNINVITED GUEST

A killer retreat

K.T. GALLOWAY

An O'Malley & Swift Thriller

ONE LAST BREATH

K.T. GALLOWAY

An O'Malley & Swift Thriller

STILL WATERS

K.T. GALLOWAY

Printed in Great Britain
by Amazon